ME AND JASPER

The one truth – maybe the only truth – I ever knew for sure is that no friend in this world could face down unnatural forces with the strength and conviction of my friend Jasper Bohanon. And how. Me and Jasper, we've seen a hell of a lot of weirdness in our ninety-something years together on this planet, but as long as I had him at my back it felt like we could pull through just about anything.

And we did, too. We just about did.

It might go against mankind's common instinct to say this, but then again me and Jasper never did consider ourselves the common sort, so saying it's just what I'm gonna do. In my adventures with Jasper Bohanon – the adventures we've had already and the adventures I know we'll find soon enough – I've learned a single fact above all others: there are things out there in the shadows, waiting on us. Cold things. Dead things. Awful, evil things, things that reach out from the shadows and grab your throat, things that would just as soon shred the skin from your bones as look at you with their one good eye. Things damned to hell forever. Things that ain't supposed to be real. Things that would stay out of the light forever if most men had their way.

But me and Jasper, we aren't most men.

This is the story of how we walked in the darkness...

ISBN-13:
978-0692520833 (Point Nine Publishing)

ISBN-10:
069252083X

10 9 8 7 6 5 4 3 2 1
FIRST EDITION, August 2015
by Point Nine Publishing

ADVENTURES IN TERROR

BOOK ONE

Mostly the 1980s

POINT NINE PUBLISHING

To "Uncle" Bob Martin, Tony Timpone, Stephen King, and Joe Lansdale. They may never read this book, but without them, it's doubtful anybody else would have, either.

In memory of Steven Goldmann.

Table of Contents

PART ONE

DEATH RATTLE

"It was in their friendship they just wanted to run forever, shadow and shadow."

Ray Bradbury, *Something Wicked This Way Comes*

THE DEATH RATTLE OF THE TWENTIETH CENTURY

Time travel is real. Real as anything else ever dreamed up by men.

You'll see.

My name is Grady Strange Claremont VII. That's right, the seventh. You don't see that much anymore, the seventh in a line. Hell, you barely see a third. Much as I hate to say it, there's just nowhere near the same level of respect for tradition with folks these days as when I was growing up almost a hundred years ago, in the gauzy old days of the 1980s and '90s. Or, as I like to refer to that period, the death rattle of the twentieth century.

If that sounds like a long time ago, it was. There's no denying it. No matter how much we might tell ourselves as we get older that we still "feel young," that "forty's not that old" or fifty or sixty either, there comes a certain point where age is just that: age. More than a number. More than a feeling. And when you're pushing towards a whole century's worth of age, brother, you're old no matter how you feel.

So, yes, I grew up in mostly the 1980s and that was a long time ago. Truth.

Here's more truth: one thing you'll learn as you grow up in this world is that the more time passes, the faster it gets.

You start off as a kid, thinking about old age like it's some distant end point on a line and you ain't ever gonna reach it. Then you start moving along that line – slow enough at first, plenty of time to watch all the scenery – and pretty soon the thought occurs, maybe that end point ain't so distant after all. You're heading towards it. It's real.

Then you start moving faster. And the more you move down that line, the faster everything gets. The scenery whips by. The days whip by. The years whip by. Your life whips by.

Somewhere along the way, a funny thing happens. As you get closer to the end of your time, life slows down again. Years, days, minutes, seconds. You end up face to face with your younger days, like you're running on a grand curve, circling back towards where everything started in your life. How did that happen? You don't know. You don't care. You're looking at your youth again. All that matters is everything you've ever had, and you aren't about to let go now.

That's time travel.

Like I told you, time travel is real.

Real as anything else ever dreamed up by men.

We'll talk more about that later.

Anyway, tradition.

Around these parts, Claremont is something of an uncommon name. There's a lot of Smiths and Johnsons and more than a few Wilsons – Townsends and Holders, too – but there's never been many Claremonts. I believe it's French in origin. Most people in this part of the country are German and English immigrants all up and down their family tree.

Like a lot of people around here, I was named after my father, and my father's father, and my father's father's father. Where I'm from, we like to pass the best parts of ourselves down through the generations. Dad always told me there wasn't anything better a man could pass along than his own good name, and he sure did a heck of a job passing mine to me.

I never had a son though. While I suppose I'll be the last of the Grady Strange Claremonts, I sure like to think I've done right by all the Claremonts who came before me.

DUST

Now, I'm deep into my ninth decade. I sure never thought I'd live long enough to say that out loud, but here I am.

You can believe me or you can not believe me, whichever you want, but here's what I want to tell you more than anything: I was a young man once, prone to fighting. Yes, me. A fighter. It ain't something I'm all that proud of but it ain't something I run away from, neither. My life's road just forked off in a fighting direction and I followed wherever it went, kicking and spitting the whole time.

Now, I'm damn near a hundred years old, and ain't kicked more than gravel dust in a decade. That's just how it is. Sooner or later you'll be headed towards a hundred yourself and you won't kick much then, either. You think you will, but you won't. You touch a century and your dancing days are long gone, I can just about promise you that.

HOME

Of course, I haven't always been ninety-something years old and if you want to get right down to it, I used to be a lot younger. I was even eleven years old once, odd as such a notion might seem to those of you kids who think old men like me come out of the womb ready to cash a Social Security check, with bones that break like candy canes, and silvery hair already thinning on our heads.

But I wasn't born this way. I *was* eleven once. I really was. I swear.

My early days were spent in the knobby hills of Eastern Kentucky, on the fringe of a dime-sized town called Whistle Mill. Back then, Whistle Mill was a spit-wad of a place that didn't have the good sense to burn itself down after the last train left, following a big logging boom that swept through the area during the gauzy amber tones of the way-back 1890s. These days it ain't much better. It just sits there spoiling on the east end of Seward County like a bad bunch of bananas, nine miles or so from the county seat of Sewardville.

Sewardville lies on the west side of the county. Maybe you've heard about it. It's the first incorporated town that eastbound travelers encounter as they descend the East Kentucky Parkway into the depths of Appalachia. The county government buildings are all there, too – the courthouse, the fire department, the sheriff and such. There are some fast food restaurants, and the county's only high school and middle school. Folks fly their stars and stripes every federal holiday at least, and some fly them every day. The last Saturday of every April, just about the whole county comes out for the Orchid Festival, Seward County's one true claim to fame. The show brings visitors from around the state – not to mention the border parts of West Virginia and Ohio – to see the orchids in all their shapes and colors.

(They especially come for the famous *Orchistradae Mountain*, better known as the mountain orchid. The mountain orchid's got long white petals with wispy cups on each end, and the petals droop down in pairs that cling together at the tips. A lot of folks say it looks for all the world like tiny hands clasped in prayer. Maybe that sounds silly but you'll believe it when you see it.)

Yessir. Life might be a little slow around the Sewardville end of Seward County, but I think if you asked most folks living there, they'd tell you that's just the way they like it. It's about as Main Street U.S.A. as you can find these crazy days.

Then, on the other hand, there's Whistle Mill. That's where I grew up.

Main Street U.S.A, Whistle Mill is not.

Whistle Mill's a little further off the path, the sort of town where a person's gotta *want* to get there to actually get there. It's a twisty drive up state Highway 15. After you leave Sewardville, you head towards the top of the ridge, run along it for a good piece, and then come back down again as the road settles along the base of some foothill mountains. Muddy tobacco and soybean fields on your left and dark walls of glistening, wet clay on your right where they cut the road through the bottom of the hill. You drive, and there ain't nothing for a while, not a house or a barn or a gas station one, until out pops a little I.G.A. grocery. When you see that I.G.A., you're in Whistle Mill.

I like to think of Whistle Mill as being the opposite of Sewardville. Sewardville sits out in the open, right off the Parkway exit ramp, with wide streets lit up by convenience store and fast food signs. Pizza Hut, Wendy's, McDonald's, Taco Bell. Shell, Pilot, Valero. Nothing to hide.

Whistle Mill... it hides.

Sort of sits in the shadows.

Likes it back there.

The place ain't much, but then again, it ain't trying to be much. Home to just under four hundred salt-of-the-earth people, the Mill ain't no more than a couple streets' worth of houses and the occasional small business establishment, if a customer or two a week actually constitutes "business." A metal shop here, a lawn mower repair place there. They renamed a straight stretch of Highway 15 as Maple Street, and that cuts the main drag through town.

There's not a whole lot going on by way of gainful employment, but then again, these days places like Whistle Mill aren't much more than bedroom communities anyway. Folks with big jobs work up the parkway in Winchester, or even further on down I-64, all the way to Lexington.

Hate to say it, but a few more businesses called Whistle Mill home when I grew up than do now. A couple enterprises that sprung up in the Mill during World War II somehow managed to get a decent run of it. They employed fifty or sixty people each. One manufactured sheet metal screws, the other made nails and staples. I figure that at one point Whistle Mill had to be the small-fastener capital of Eastern Kentucky and if anybody ever bothered looking it up I'd bet the facts would probably have backed me up on that.

Now there's not much of anything. As a matter of fact the only one that's survived more or less intact all these years is the I.G.A. grocery. A little gas station on the opposite end of town was a Sunoco in my day but since then it's also been a Chevron, a BP, and a Texaco. Nowadays it's just called Stanley's, named for the guy who owns it. All the national energy conglomerates pulled out of little towns decades ago, leaving us to fend for ourselves. Oh well.

Whistle Mill Elementary sits on a hill a mile or so past Stanley's, with kids bused in from the outlying hollers to fill out all the classrooms. The school's been remodeled and rebuilt five or six times since I was a student there, but it's still in the same general spot. They've even got the same wrought iron merry-go-round that I played on as a kindergartner. I do get a kick out of that.

People in Whistle Mill are about as friendly as you might expect – friendly as it gets back in the shadows, anyway. Everybody waves at each other, whether they're passing in cars or sitting in their yards watching the fireflies dance against the orange light of dusk.

The citizens don't smile too much, though. I'm here to tell you right now so if you ever come to visit you don't think it's just you. It's not just you. They really don't smile too much at all in Whistle Mill and that's just how it is. Most folks keep a look on their face that's halfway between a frown and a sick stomach. That's not to say everybody stays in a bad mood; it's just they look a little irritated most times. There's a bunch of reasons why and we'll get into them soon enough.

Still, most everyone waves at everyone else. I suppose it's proper manners.

Sour looks or no, for the most part, everybody around town will tell you, there ain't much to worry about in Whistle Mill. They'll tell you that. Most of the houses stay unlocked, day or night. There's a break-in on occasion, a brick through a window, one person taking a swing at another, little happenings here and there. Nobody frets too much, though; the Mill's got a way of fixing its own problems.

I said there ain't much to Whistle Mill on the surface, and I meant it. Just those nice folks, flying their American flags and waving at each other every morning, while they gaze at the rest of the world with an expression that would lead you to believe they were on the verge of one bad case of the runs.

That's the surface, though. That's what everybody sees.

Beneath the surface, though... that's different.

There's a little more to Whistle Mill down there in the places where you can't see without shining a little extra lamplight. Like I said, it sits back in the shadows, and I figure that as long as there's a Whistle Mill in this corner of the map, it's gonna live in darkness. That's true – it just is. True in ways that most folks never see or even think about, true in ways that most people never even consider as possibility, true in ways that most would never even *want* to consider.

After all, sometimes it's just easier not to believe.

JASPER

Let's talk a little more about the here and now.

Tonight's the first night of autumn. Autumn is my favorite season, but then again I reckon it's most people's favorite season. The moon's throwing pale blue light across most of the earth, but out here, around my house, no more than a few jaggy beams making it through the tree tops. There's a sharp edge to the air. I live a mile or so outside of town and out here fog creeps out of the woods behind the house, hovering above the dewy grass like a death shroud.

I'm watching that fog roll in from my seat on the back porch, the same wicker rocking chair I take up most every night. Soon, it'll be the witching hour. I don't know what that'll bring, but it'll probably bring something. Seems like it usually does around these parts.

Some folks say ninety-nine's a mite old to be outside on an October night like tonight, with fog tendrils hanging around the yard and the air temperature hovering just under forty degrees. Anybody that knows me, though, knows I ain't never been "some folks." I might have left behind my vibrant youth but I still got most everything else right here with me. Always liked a nip in the fresh evening air, and if it pleases you to hear, I don't feel like giving that up just because I crossed whatever imaginary age line the younger folks believe divvies people into those who can take care of themselves, and those who can't.

I can take care of myself. Take care of myself just fine. So what if my blood don't run as hot as it used to? All I gotta do is throw a blanket around my shoulders, wrap my hands around a cup of hot coffee – I take mine black as a spade flush – and I can get along just fine.

Besides, I ain't got enough nights left on Earth to waste, no how. I'm all too aware that those nights I do have are precious. Precious indeed. No need spending them stiff, parked in front of a TV screen, watching the news and muttering thoughts aloud to my many invisible pals. I'd much rather sit alone and stare at the far-off stars, pondering the darkness between and beyond, the great black forever that waits for us all.

I find myself pondering that forever a lot. The older I get, the more I think about it. I doubt I'm much different than anyone else in that regard.

A lot of soulful thoughts come to me on these nights. I often find myself sharing philosophies with the dead, so to speak. Most of it comes down to one single solitary point: there's a reckoning coming my way. I know it. Sure as hell, there ain't a damned thing I or anybody else can do to stop it. The reckoning comes when it comes. Seems to me that worrying about the whens and whys of the future is as much of a time waster as sitting in front of that television and letting my brain drip like so much useless mush.

I ain't afraid of what's out there, but that don't mean I ain't thinking about it more with every day that passes. Figure I'll just sit here on this porch with my blanket and my coffee, and wait for it to come.

In the meantime, my letters keep me busy.

Hey Grady,

I suppose that I should apologize for not writing to you in a few months. I meant no offense. With everything that's brought us to this point, I figured it was probably best to just lay low for a while and let the universe chase us for once, instead of us chasing after it like we have for all these years. We've stirred up plenty of adventures in our day; I've been thinking that maybe this is the time to finally let it all settle back down.

It seems like more and more I find myself thinking that maybe we've finally outrun it all. Do you ever think that? Sometimes at night, I sit here at my kitchen table, looking out the window, towards the night sky. Do you know what I see out there? Infinity, Grady. Just like we always talked about. Infinity in all its wonder and beauty, swirling around its own center, folding in and around and through itself, through everything and nothing all at the same time. When we were younger I'd look up at that sky and think about all the terrors and marvels that must be waiting up there. Now, I look up and wonder how much longer it will be before we join them ourselves.

What about you, my friend? Wait, don't tell me. Not yet. I will visit soon and we can talk about it then.

As always,
Jasper

It's been almost a month since Jasper sent me that letter, and I've lost count of how many hundreds of times I've pulled the single sheet of yellow stationery from the envelope, read his words, and gently folded them back up and tucked them away again until the next time. I'm always careful not to damage the thin paper. It's almost as rare as the thought it contains; most folks don't use the regular Post at all anymore, but Jasper insists on it. *Letter writing is an art form and I hope it never dies.* He's said that to me more than once.

Much as I hate to say it, I don't hear from Jasper much these days. I miss that. Do I ever. We talk from time to time and even find a chance to visit in person on rare occasion, but nothing like back in the magic times when our rowdy adventures were at their all-out rowdiest. I guess we've learned the simple but sad fact of the matter: the older you get, the more you drift. On through the ages, on through infinity. Even though me and him were close as Band-Aids and arm hairs for all those years – damn near every bit of our nine decades so far on this Earth – I suppose it's true that in the end, the drift got us just as the same as it gets everybody else.

Like I said before, I was a fighter in my younger days. It's the honest truth. Fought everything coming and going, sometimes twice just to be sure. I never met nothing or nobody that could back me down and I'm pretty sure that if such a thing existed it would've shown itself by now. I've whipped about everything there is to whip at least once and some more than that, but

I'd be lying if I said I did it all by myself. And I don't like lying.

There's a lot I can tell you about Jasper James Bohanon, and a lot I *will* tell you about him. Soon enough. But for now, just know this: Jasper was sharp like an icicle, and could come off just as cold, too, if you didn't know how to take him, which of course most people didn't. He was the smartest guy I ever knew, and the meanest. Mean as a striped snake. Not mean like he wanted to hurt people, but mean like he wouldn't let anybody hurt *him*. At his tallest he couldn't quite see the top of a refrigerator and he never packed more than a hundred and sixty pounds on his wiry frame, not even when age and junk food was getting the best of the rest of us, but it didn't matter. He was that tough.

In all my days I never saw anything human or otherwise get the best of Jasper Bohanon. I surely did not. And believe you me, plenty took their best shot.

The first of those times – at least the first one that I ever saw – happened in the summer of nineteen hundred and eighty-six. We were ten years old, newly freed from the confines of elementary school, staring at sixth grade like we were looking straight down the barrel of a twelve gauge Browning shotgun. Just stupid enough to believe we'd already figured out a thing or two about this world. I'm guessing you probably know how that worked out, which is to say, it worked out for us the same way it works out for anybody else. Which of course *that* is to say, we learned otherwise.

But *how* we learned, well now, that's a story worth telling. Maybe I got enough time left to tell it before my reckoning comes, maybe I don't, but if you just sit with me a spell, we'll find out together.

I remember it went something like this...

ME AND JASPER AND THE SUMMER OF '86

Me and Jasper sat there smack dab in the sticky July midnight. We were trapped. Trapped, and helpless, deep within the tangled woods that stretched outside of Whistle Mill, Kentucky. Around us, the acrid smell of death swirled into the summertime atmosphere like motor oil pouring into dog piss. It was the summer of nineteen hundred and eighty-six, and right about that moment, I wondered if it might be the last summer the two of us boys would ever see.

The smell. God, the smell. You ever experience a smell that actually sticks to you? A smell that crawls up your nose and lodges itself in the depths of the olfactory nerves, such a powerful smell that you never get all the way rid of it, not for the rest of your life, not for nothing, no matter how hard you try? I have. It's funny how some details stay with you, especially details from those Big moments – and trust me, what I'm about to tell you, it *was* a Big moment. But what comes to mind more than anything about that evening is that damned odor: hot, and sick, and nasty. Horrible. Saying it smelled like meat rotting on a countertop might get you started, but it wouldn't take you all the way down the road, if you know what I mean.

The smell hung around us, oppressive, brutal. And it meant only one thing.

The banshee was out there.

She had us, if she wanted. We weren't moving. Not so much as a muscle, not so much as a hair, not so much as a popcorn fart. We were too scared to move even if we wanted.

The full moon dangled high over our heads, rolling silver off the still waters of Boone Creek. I was puckered up so tight that John Henry himself couldn't have knocked a greased BB up my ass with his mighty railroad sledgehammer. From the way Jasper's eyes was about to bust out of their sockets I felt pretty sure that he wasn't doing any better.

The two of us crouched beneath an overhang at the edge of the creek bank, backs pressed against a slimy limestone wall. We didn't have no place to go, couldn't have got anywhere if we did know where to go.

Above our heads, the pale lady floated.

She hovered a couple feet from the rock ledge - not back, not forth, just there. Just there, like she was waiting but didn't know what for, like she was watching for somebody and didn't know when they might come. The whole time she never made a sound – not a whisper, not a cry. Still I knew that sooner or later, her haunted wail would come; I just wasn't so sure that I wanted to be there when it did. Which was funny, because five hours earlier I'd have sworn my life's mission was tracking this banshee and meeting her head on.

That wasn't my mission anymore, though.

Getting me and my friend out of there alive was all that worried me in that moment.

If you know anything about banshees, anything at all, you can probably bring up a good picture in your mind. When we first saw this one, back in the woods a couple hundred yards from the creek, I thought she looked pretty much like what I had seen in my storybooks. Everything about her was pale white, even the soft glow that enveloped her from top to bottom. She was tall, a good foot and a half taller than any woman I'd ever seen, and twice as thin, too. Her long, stringy hair danced outward from her head just like it was floating in water. Her arms and hands shimmied out in the same manner, white ribbons ever reaching for someone that would come to her soon enough.

"You know they're a death harbinger," Jasper had told me earlier, *"come calling for unfortunate souls who're marked for leaving this world and on to the next one. If the souls ain't quite ready to go, the banshee stays around, haunting the grounds, just waiting until time's up, and when that final death moment comes they let off the god-awfullest scream, like they want the angels up in Heaven to know they're on their way. Or the devils down in hell."*

I'd looked at him real strange when he said that. Back in those days, I didn't know what "harbinger" meant.

I figured it out soon enough.

Anyway, me or Jasper neither one wanted to draw the banshee's scream now. From where we sat, I couldn't make out her face but it seemed like she was gazing out towards the woods on the other side of the creek. What she was looking for, we didn't know, not yet anyway. Oh, we'd find out eventually. Sure we would. But for now, all we could see was the tail of her white dress dancing out over the edge of the rock and into the night. A thin wisp of ghost cloth drifted gentle on the warm wind, only there wasn't no wind to speak of. Then, she drifted out across the water. And there we were.

I tend to catalogue my past years by which movies were released in each one, and thinking back on it now, it's clear to me that nineteen eighty-six was twelve months for the history books.

That year saw a ton of all-time classics. *ALIENS* came out in theaters, and so did *The Fly*, the one with Jeff Goldblum. Not the one where Vincent Price swapped his noggin and one hand with a housefly. I'm talking about the one where Jeff Goldblum teleported himself across his apartment and ended up a fly himself, sort of a fly anyway, the real gross-out kind, with an all-time case of back acne and his nuts and fingernails in a medicine cabinet. You know. *That* version. One of the true classics.

You'd be awful hard pressed to find a sane person who'd claim that *The Fly* and *ALIENS* didn't kick more ass than a monkey with one leg tied over its little monkey head. *ALIENS* is pure action horror spectacle, all space marines and huge plasma cannons and queen-alien-ripping-androids-in-half attitude. *The Fly* is spectacle, too, maybe not quite the level of action as the space marines but definitely featuring a lot more scenes of Jeff Goldblum using the bathroom medicine cabinet for storage of sundry body parts. Also, he pukes acid. A lot. For extra kicks there's a giant maggot in there somewhere, too.

Just by the measure of those two movies, nineteen eighty-six would have been a banner year, but Hollywood saw fit to spread the wealth even more. Also in nineteen eighty-six, the world received *Texas Chainsaw Massacre 2,* featuring the return of Leatherface, and *Friday the 13ᵗʰ Part VI: Jason Lives,* featuring the first appearance of zombie Jason Voorhees. We got *Poltergeist 2,* starring that crazy old preacher that looked like a relative of the Westboro Baptist patriarch, and we also got *Big Trouble in Little China*, which was directed by John Carpenter at the top of his game, and to this day might be the movie I re-watch more than any other.

On the non-horror side, there was *Top Gun, Ferris Bueller's Day Off, Platoon, Stand by Me* – legit classics. There was *Crocodile Dundee,* and of course, *Star Trek IV: The Voyage Home*, with Mr. Spock giving the Vulcan death grip to punk rockers and mind melding with humpback whales at Sea World. But like I said, all that was on the non-horror side, and as you'll come to find out I don't much concern myself with the non-horror side. There's plenty enough horror in this world to keep me busy, after all.

*

Me and Jasper Bohanon met in the fifth grade, and I remember those years clear and clean, like they was playing out again right in front of me. The way some might remember their college years or others might recall their wedding day and their firstborn child, that's how I remember my first days with Jasper. I never had a wife, and I sure ain't had no college, but by hell, I had some adventures with my friend Jasper, and when it comes to pivotal life moments I'd put those up against yours anytime.

It was actually 1985 when me and Jasper first crossed paths, the week before Halloween to be exact, in Mrs. Beechcraft's class at Whistle Mill Elementary. As it turned out, that was quite a coincidental week for us to meet. Some might even call it destiny, seeing as how just a few days after we met, we both celebrated our first eleven years on Earth: I was born a minute before midnight, October thirtieth, and Grady come into the world one minute after midnight, on Halloween. Way back in the gauzy old days of nineteen hundred seventy-sour. How about that. The two of us, brought into this world back to back.

Since we were both born so late in the fall, we were older than most of the kids in our class at school. Even if it was by just a few months, it made a difference, and I've always believed that was one reason we hit it off so fast. Sometimes, you can just tell when things fit right.

I'd just moved in from the other side of the county, and didn't much care for making friends, partly because I had better to do than introduce myself to the other kids, partly because the other kids had better to do than introduce themselves to me. I didn't have any quarrel with that. Far as I could tell, my *X-Men, G.I. Joe,* and *ROM: Spaceknight* comic books were all the friends I needed, along with a collector case full of G.I. Joe and Star Wars action figures and the occasional *Fangoria* magazine (THE #1 HORROR MAGAZINE!, it said right there on the cover), which at the time was severe contraband on account of most of the kids was still watching Disney cartoons and all of the teachers tended to get downright uppity about full-color pictures of exploding heads and hacked-off arms or legs, even if it *was* just movie magic.

I kept to myself and my comic books the first few days in my new school, just like I had in my old school and just like I did most everywhere else, too. But soon enough, it came to my attention that there was someone sharing my interests, a kid over in Mr. Gilmore's fifth grade class, and I might want to get acquainted with him.

That was Jasper. Up to the point we met, I'd steered clear of everybody at my new elementary school, and felt pretty good about it. I didn't bother them and they didn't bother me, which worked out all right far as I was concerned.

Then, the Wednesday before Halloween, I was reading the latest *X-men* at recess, back rested against the school wall, when I looked up for just a second and saw a skinny, brown-haired kid with a bowl cut and wire-rimmed glasses playing in the dirt by himself maybe thirty feet from where I stood. When I say skinny, I mean his arms were no bigger around than a rake handle and his legs weren't much more than that, either. He appeared to be three or four inches taller than me, too, and since I was already bigger than most of the kids in this new school, that meant he was taller than *all* of them.

It's funny now, the way eventually puberty caught up with everybody and Jasper went from being the tallest kid in school to one of the smallest. But back then, he stood out big time. It struck me that being that tall and that skinny made him look lonelier. I ain't sayin' he *was* that lonely, but he sure did look that part. He stood out on the playground like a weed grown out of a sidewalk, swaying in the slightest breeze.

Out there underneath a wide oak tree, he had a couple little figurines in each hand and was bouncing them off each other hard as he could. Even from a distance I could tell for certain that they were G.I. Joes – Duke, Destro, and two Cobra soldiers, to be exact. He had a Skeletor from Masters of the Universe, too, but it lay off lonely to one side, which also was a good sign because I never had a lot of that gang myself. Beast-man, Mer-Man, Stinkor. Out of my league.

Long story short, I went over there.

"Hi," I said. "My name's Grady." I noticed that his Destro flopped loose at the waist, where the rubber o-ring had worn out from too much play. Another good sign.

Jasper raised both eyebrows and sucked down a long, slow breath, which I come to learn was what he did whenever he found the subject at hand especially peculiar. He didn't say anything, though.

"You all right?" I tried again.

He didn't answer.

I took a step back, and turned to retreat across the playground. Then, at last, he spoke up. "Grady, huh?"

"Yeah," I said. "Nice to meet you." I extended a hand in friendship, but he didn't immediately take it.

After a couple of seconds, though, Jasper reached up and accepted my offer. "Well, huh," he said, and we shook on that, even though he never took his eyes off that flippy-flop Destro figure.

"What kind of name's Grady?" he asked, still not looking up.

"It's the name they gave me," I said.

"Really?"

"Yeah, really."

"Who did?"

"Who did what?"

"Who gave it to you?"

"My Mom and Dad. Who do you think?"

I wasn't sure if it was a trick question. While I pondered, he shrugged one shoulder and said, "Jasper's the name mine gave me."

"I never met anybody named Jasper," I said.

Well, truth be told, there was a kid back at my old school whose great grandpa was named Jasper, but I never actually met him, so there you go.

"It's an alright name," he explained. And for the first time, he looked up at me. "I heard worse. I'm gonna call you Boo, OK?"

"Boo? What for?"

"Because it's better than Grady," he said. "You ain't got much of a name is all. I ain't trying to be mean, but truth is if I was you I'd hate that name and I'd tell my Mom and Dad about it, too. I'd probably spend a lot of time wondering about what I could change it to whenever I got old enough to head down to the courthouse and do something about it. Maybe that's just me, though."

I shrugged, and sat down cross-legged on the ground. "OK then," I said. "Whatever jangles your dangle."

He laughed.

That was our first conversation. Not normally my style – me being more of the quiet type – but sometimes when you know about folks, you just know.

Soon enough I found out that not only did Jasper own a lot of Joes, he also was into comic books and Star Wars and Indiana Jones.

Best of all, he had a stack of *Fangoria* magazines in his satchel, too! I saw the covers poking out, almost like they *wanted* to be seen. That sharp logo at the top, the filmstrip style graphic down one side with a gnarly little movie picture in each cell. Heck yes. *It's Alive!, Dawn of the Dead*. Heck yes. *Friday the 13th*. *Nightmare on Elm Street*. *Gremlins*. Heck yes. *Evil Dead*. Heck yes. *Fright Night*. Heck yes. *Re-Animator*. HECK YES.

"Where'd you get *those?*" I gasped, pointing at the *Fangoria*s like they were a sack full of hundred dollar bills.

"One place or another. Places where I get stuff. You know." Jasper shrugged. As I'd soon find out, he shrugged at most matters in life. He could shrug to put a teenage girl to shame. He was a world renowned shrugger.

I stared at Jasper's magazines for what felt like three days. Ain't ashamed to say, I'd have given everything I had and half of what I didn't to find out where he got them. It looked to my eyes like he might have every issue of *Fangoria* ever printed. Far as I was concerned, this was something like looking at a unicorn.

Then...

BOOM.

Buried in his collection, with just one dog-eared corner stuck out, was the *Fangoria* that ruled all other *Fangoria*s. The one I desired like man desired to reach the stars, like Romeo desired Juliet, like Johnny Cash desired June Carter, like Roscoe P. Coletrain and Boss Hogg desired to one day run down them Dukes, them Dukes. At that point, I'd been trying to get my hands on this particular issue for a good three or four years, or I should say, get my hands on it *again*.

Issue Number Nine.

Folks, we are talking about the Ark of the Covenant here. Ask anybody that knows anything about *Fangoria* and scary flicks and bad ass horror material in general and they'll back me up on this.

Actually you don't need to ask, because I'm telling you right now: issue number nine – Issue Number Nine, it needs all capital letters – featured the infamous *Motel Hell* cover. You probably heard about it: that farmer dude in denim overalls and red flannel shirt, wearing a severed pig head for a helmet, wielding a bloody chainsaw like it was the mighty Excalibur or something. Far as I was concerned, human hands wasn't capable of creating a more badass cover. Probably they still aren't.

The sad part is, though, that cover was so bad ass, it didn't take too long before a few so-called "adult" peckerwoods jumped up on their high horses and got it banned from every drugstore and supermarket in the country. Let me say that again: *that cover was so bad ass, the peckerwoods got it declared unfit for human consumption.* Pulled from stores. Burnt up on the sacrificial fires of common decency, as some folks say.

So yeah. Apparently a few grannies in Alabama – while I don't know if it was really Alabama, Alabama sounds likely as any place – stumbled across that particular Fangoria down at the Piggly Wiggly or the beauty shop or wherever old grannies stumbled across random shit, and this indeed caused their plastic panties to get all wadded up in such a manner that I had never experienced before in my life (at least up to that point, anyway). If you know anything, you know how the story goes whenever grannies get their panties in a wad.

The issue escalates.

The righteous grannies pitched a fit to their preacher, a man of great wisdom and humility who immediately got on the line to the Reverend Jimmy Swaggart. The good ol' Rev Jimmy kept a few friends in high places – this was back in the days when some people actually gave a rip what Jimmy Swaggart had to say about anything – and so the Reverend picked up the telephone and called his coonskin-hat-wearing buddy Pat Buchanan (no time to explain, just look it up), who had some connections with the White House (yes, that White House) and even ended up working there a little after this story takes place.

Of course back then, the White House was occupied – some would say graced by the ethereal presence of – one Ronald Wilson Reagan, otherwise known as the Gipper, otherwise known as Uncle Ronnie otherwise known as He Who Walks Behind the Rows. Folks called him the Gipper because that was a movie role he played during his Hollywood days, and they called him Uncle Ronnie because by golly, he was just so down home and sweet that everybody wanted him in the family. I called him He Who Walks Behind the Rows because that was the devil in a Stephen King short story called "Children of the Corn" and it seemed pretty dang apt to me for reasons that don't need to be discussed here. But I digress.

Okay. Soon enough, Pat did as the Reverend Jimmy Swaggart requested, and bent the blessed ear of the almighty President Reagan, telling him about all the ruckus being raised by the God-fearing people of the U.S. of A. When Saint Reagan heard that, he bent down and kissed the ground and farted, and declared that Issue Number Nine of *Fangoria* was inflicting evil on the minds of innocent little Ronnies all throughout the golden land, and therefore must be yanked off every shelf in the country, if not the world, if not the whole trickle down damn universe. So he said, and so it was.

Well, that's the story I always heard, at least. I can't swear to it, but that's what I heard.

Anyway, despite the Reaganistas' efforts, a few hundred copies escaped. Somehow one of them ended up at Comic Book Land in Lexington, Kentucky, and miraculous as it may seem, happened to be sitting on the shelf one of the rare Saturdays that I visited the store. I was headed for the back issue bins when I glanced over at the New Arrivals rack and saw it gleaming.

I couldn't get my hands on it fast enough, let me just tell you. Soon as I did, I took it back to Mom and said, "Mom, this is what I'm getting today. No *X-Men*. No *Captain America*. No *Spider-man*." This was a couple of years before *ROM* and *G.I. Joe* came out, but I would have walked away from them that day, too.

All I wanted was that one issue of *Fangoria*, Issue Number Nine, with the chainsaw dude in overalls and a dead pig mask.

So I said, "Mom, this is what I'm getting."

She studied the cover for a few seconds, gave bloody pig head guy a good once-over, and said, "No sir, you most certainly are not."

"But mom, he's got overalls and a dead pig head and his chainsaw's got blood on it –"

"I said you're not getting it."

"No, Mom, *you're* the one not getting it –"

"Put it back."

"Come on, Mom –"

"Put it back. *Now.*"

Good thing I had a backup plan. One rule I always follow is: never give up hope. If you ain't got hope you might as well lay down in the street and wait for the ice cream truck to run over your sorry but. I took that *Fangoria* and stuck it in the middle of some *Wonder Woman* back issues, figuring it would be safe there since Wonder Woman sucks and nobody was gonna be looking in that box any time soon. That would give me a few weeks to convince Mom that I should get that *Fangoria,* and when I did convince her I could just pluck it out of the *Wonder Woman*s on the next trip.

It wasn't meant to be. The next time I visited Comic Book Land, the *Wonder Woman*s were still there but my *Fangoria* was long gone. I still haven't figured out how that happened, but it did. Jimmy Swaggart and Ronald Reagan ruined the fun for everybody.

*

In the years since, I often thought about my close encounter with Issue Number Nine, but not until that moment on the playground with Jasper had I gotten a real whiff of another copy. Remember, this was way before your average two year old child could hit Ebay and find anything he wants in the seconds it takes to type in a search box. Which, by the way, takes a whole lot of the fun out of collecting as far as I'm concerned but that's a whole other discussion. I could go there right now and find a hundred copies of Issue Number Nine and probably not pay more than three dollars for all of them together. But if I do that, this story's not near as much worth telling.

Anyhow, Jasper reached into that satchel and sure as the world, pulled *Fangoria* Number Nine out without me even asking! I saw that chainsaw, that pig head, and those overalls, right there on paper, not five feet away, and I swear my heart did a jig.

"You... you care if I borrow that?" I asked, a little bit nervous.

"Have at it," he said. Then he handed it over without a hesitation.

I took the magazine and felt like a horse in hay for doing it. After another few minutes, I bent down in the dirt and picked up a couple of Jasper's G.I. Joe figures. Not long after that, we started playing as though we'd been playing together since the day we crawled out of the crib.

From that point on, every day we'd spend half of recess talking scary movies or comic books, and the other half matching up my preferred Gung Ho/Snake-Eyes team against Jasper's Stormshadow/Firefly and see who could kick the most ass in fifteen minutes.

For the rest of fifth grade, for thirty minutes we was G.I. Joe and *Fangoria* buddies, and when you're ten years old that's an important buddy to have. Still, it was just thirty minutes; after that, I went back to Mrs. Beechcraft and he went back to Mr. Gilmore and that was it until the next day.

Yeah, we hit it off. Pretty good, I'd say. But the truth is, we didn't really and truly became *friends* until a few months later, during the summer of '86. It was right before we moved on to the county middle school. That was the first time in my life I saw some stuff which far as I'm concerned just ain't meant to be seen by boys of a certain age, no matter how bad ass those boys might consider themselves.

Make no mistake, we were Bad Ass as they come. Thought we were, anyway. But looking back, it's almost comical. Jeez. We were ten years old. Ten years old. I don't know. I just... I don't know.

Okay, I do know. You know, I know, we all know. When you're that age, you just aren't ready to face the world. You think you are, sure. You think you got it all handled, that you can whup whatever the world throws at you and barely break a sweat doing it. But you're ten years old, and you *ain't* ready, and it don't matter what you think. That's just how it is.

*

We watched the Boone Creek banshee float over our heads. Across the black water she went, the wispy tails of her gown floating at her back like eerie wings. I noticed that the moonlight never broke so much as a ripple on the water's surface even when she passed right through the hoary beams. She moved towards the bank, back up the wooded hillside and touched nothing but air the whole time. Never turned and looked towards me and Jasper, either. We realized she wasn't out for us, which made it a little easier to breathe.

As the eerie girl vanished into the trees, I whispered to my friend, "Do you think she's gone for good?"

"Nah," he said. "She'll be back soon enough. She ain't going nowhere. Not 'til she gets what she came for, anyway."

"What do you think that was?" I asked.

"Not what. Who."

I looked at him. He looked at me. Neither of us cared to know that answer.

We crawled out from under the rock overhang, and walked out on a gravelly spit that edged up to the creek, stepping slow so that when the pebbles shifted under our feet, it didn't make too much noise. The last thing we wanted was that banshee coming back after us.

Off in the distance, way back towards the highway, I could hear Uncle Teddy coming. Actually it wasn't so much Uncle Teddy as it was those two coonhounds of his, stirring through the brush. Homer and Henry. That was their names.

Uncle Teddy always said they were two of the finest tracking dogs he'd ever owned but I doubted they ever tracked something like this before.

From all the noise they made I felt a renewed sense like maybe we weren't so safe after all. There seemed a real chance they might draw that banshee back our way. She hadn't done so much as look at us crossways yet – just sort of floated in space, watching and waiting for whatever it was she was watching and waiting for – but I figured that when it comes to dealing with a banshee, there ain't much good that can come of being in close proximity to one.

"You boys come over here?" I heard Teddy calling. "Grady? Jasper? You all hear me now?"

I started to yell back, but Jasper put a finger to my lips and shook me off. Uncle Teddy and his dogs were making noise enough already; Jasper knew that we didn't need to add to the racket.

While I was still figuring a way to draw Teddy's attention without somehow also drawing the attention of the banshee, I looked across the creek, into the woods as they disappeared up the hillside into blackness. The branches were quiet and not moving at all, but I could see a faint white glow about halfway up the hillside, headed back towards us. The pale lady in her floating gown heard the ruckus, after all. Now, she was coming back to see what all the fuss was about.

UNCLE TEDDY

Around this part of the world, the grown-ups love two things above all else: getting drunk, and telling tales. Doing both at the same time can gin up a special sort of enchantment that washes in equal waves across those who are talking, and those who are being talked to. Or, as Jasper likes to say, those who are sorcerers, and those who ain't.

It's in the quietest, gauziest darkness that the sorcery takes truest hold: the depths of midnight where the tellers of tales know there's nothing between them and you except the brief flicker of time it takes for their words to settle on the back of your neck like the icy breath of Old Scratch himself. And my, how they do conjure within those moments. If you can catch the sorcery when the campfire crackles at full blaze, when the fog rolls across the dewy fields and there's nary a sound to be heard except the sorcerer's voice and the quick breaths of those under his spell, , that's when you'll hear the best stories of all. And if you find yourself in one of those moments, then count yourself lucky – lucky, just like I've been – because brother, you caught yourself some rare magic. Believe it.

A time like that is when you'll hear tell of the Boone Creek Banshee.

Listen up, now, won't you?

I first heard about the banshee in that fateful summer of '86, during a late-night session at my Uncle Teddy Rider's place. Uncle Teddy was my mother's only brother, a rowdy sort who laughed a lot. He was four years older than Mom but acted a twenty years younger, and I enjoyed being around him. Most folks did. He stood six feet three inches tall and was about half that big around, with a grizzly beard that dangled halfway down his chest and looked to me like it was the exact color of a dry creek bed. More than once as a boy, I thought about grabbing hold of that beard and seeing if I could swing from it the way I swung from the jungle gym at school. Something tells me that if I'd ever taken the notion, Uncle Ted would have just grinned and let me go.

Teddy's kept a little building behind his house made out of concrete blocks, maybe twenty feet by twenty feet. On most weekends Mom and Dad would go up there to hang out with their friends and watch my uncle hold court, which I reckon he did better than just about anybody. That concrete building was a real storytelling sorcerer's place. Sometimes, when they couldn't get a babysitter, they'd take me along.

"Be quiet, Grady. Sit still," they'd tell me on the ride over. "If you don't be quiet and sit still, you won't get to come with us next time."

That was a serious threat, indeed. I loved going to Uncle Teddy's, listening to all those wild tales but keeping my head down so my parents thought I wasn't paying much attention. (Ha!) Mom and Dad knew I loved it, too, just like they knew I wasn't about to do anything that would endanger my visits there.

Besides, I had something to keep me occupied: my comic books.

The comics saw to it that my parents need never worry. *Uncanny X-men, New Mutants, Teen Titans. Fantastic Four.* I kept a small stack nearby at all times (and Teddy had a few older issues, too, if I ever ran short of my own). I'd read those, then re-read them, then re-read them again. Eventually it would get way past my bedtime and I'd fall asleep on the couch until time to leave.

Anyway, it was a Saturday night in July and we were up there at Teddy's when the clock flew past midnight without even saying excuse me. I felt tired but unlike most other nights I wasn't tired enough to go to sleep.

Besides, the way I looked at it, "past my bedtime" was when the adults would normally just be getting good and started with their party, and this night was no different.

They broke off in little groups of three or four, drinking beer and playing guitars or card games or whatever. I started wandering around from one group to the other, picking up little pieces of the conversations as I went. They never talked too dirty out loud, at least not when I was close by. Probably the real cussing stayed under their breath because they knew that if Mom caught one single solitary f-word within ten feet of my virgin ears, she'd pitch a fit to beat anything you ever saw. Far as what they drank – and they drank their fair share – they always told me the caramel colored liquid in their cups was ginger ale, but I knew better. It sure didn't smell like ginger ale. Anyway it was just grown-ups having fun.

Eventually I made my way over to Uncle Teddy's table, where he was holding court in the midst of a spades game. Teddy was a heck of a spades man, one of the best around. I'd heard more than a few people say that if there had been a Kentucky state championship of spades he would have won it every year for sure, and if they had a world championship he'd win that a few times, too. Maybe more than a few if they allowed a blind nil. That's how good he was.

There was about two turns left in that hand when he poked me in the shoulder and asked if I ever heard the story about Jace Watkins.

"Uh-uh," I said.

His face lit up. "Oh, you gotta hear that one. Throw this card in first," Teddy said, handing me his four of diamonds. That's why I stood at the table right next to him; I wasn't big on cards for their own sake but I always liked how Teddy would let me toss his card into the trick.

I threw it to the middle of the table, then my uncle pitched in his last card without waiting for the proper turn – I guess it was a loser – and stood up.

"All right now, folks," he said. "I need to tell a story. Apparently my nephew Grady here, he ain't never heard about what happened to ol' Jace Watkins." I felt my face turn bright red from being put on the spot and just knew everybody could see it.

And with that, Uncle Teddy launched into one of the god-awfullest stories I ever heard in my life.

Apparently Jace Watkins was a buddy of Teddy's in high school – a first cousin, actually – and the two of them used to drive around town taking care of young ladies and cans of Old Milwaukee beer in round about equal amounts.

Jace was a chunky guy with a curly blond hairdo, short on the top and long in the back, which was the style in those days even if it did look kind of comical on some guys, Jace being one. He wore a lot of AC/DC and Iron Maiden t-shirts, and somewhere along the line got his hands on a fake driver's license which he used for securing alcohol at the EZ Mart towards the county line. The way Uncle Teddy told it, Jace wasn't much to look at, but he told a good story and could make the girls laugh so he never had many dry spells, so to speak.

Now, I don't want to make this story too long. Besides, I couldn't ever tell it the way Uncle Teddy did, since he'd had years of practice. But the gist of it is, Jace Watkins was a cursed man. A Nazi rifleman sniped his granddaddy in France towards the end of World War II, then his daddy dropped dead of a brain aneurysm not three days after Jace was born, leaving Jace and his older brother to be raised by their mother. Not long after that, Jace's brother come down with leukemia. The doctors thought they caught it in time but turns out they didn't, so it was just Jace and his mama from then on.

Despite all those gray clouds hovering over his head, Jace mostly kept a good way about him. He carried himself in a pleasant sort of way and got along with just about everybody that ever crossed his path. Most folks would tell you it wasn't any surprise that he and Uncle Teddy hung out a lot.

The Saturday before they were set to graduate high school, Jace and Teddy decided to party, which they usually did decide to party on Saturdays. This one would turn out different, though. The two of them picked up a couple of girls – Marsha Johnson and Brandy Sparks, to be specific – to go with a case of Old Milwaukee and parked Jace's van in a cow pasture that butted up against Boone Creek. After they drank all the beer, Brandy decided that she had to use the bathroom, and seeing an opportunity to get one of those ladies off by herself, Jace offered to walk her out in the woods. When she said, "Okay," he said "Hot damn," and off they went.

It was the last Uncle Teddy would ever see of Jace Watkins. Leastways, it was the last he would ever see of Jace Watkins *alive*.

Jace and Brandy snuck off to the woods, leaving Teddy and Marsha in the van. Ted didn't think twice about it, since that was how they usually worked it whenever they parked with a couple of girls – one pair would keep their party in the van, the other would find a soft landing spot outside. So when Jace and Brandy flung open that van door and disappeared into the night, nobody raised their eyebrows about it. Hell, Teddy and Marsha was probably half undressed before that sliding van door ever closed back.

A few minutes later, they heard screaming.

It wasn't Brandy, though. It wasn't exactly a scream, either. It was something... else. A piercing cry. A razor blade, slashing the night. Something.

Whatever its origin, the sound shot a bolt of fear up Uncle Teddy's back unlike anything he'd ever felt before in his life.

He scrambled to get his clothes back on and find out what had happened, but by the time he got there Jace was already dead. His body lay on the ground, white as school glue, twisted up like two dogs in a knot. His dead eyes rolled all the way back, showing nothing but their lifeless whites.

Brandy stood nearby, already in shock, unable to speak. It took a few minutes before she finally managed to get any words out.

"She just took him." That's what Brandy eventually said. "Come right down and lifted Jace away, right there in front of me, like I wasn't there at all." Then she fell into hysterics, babbling and crying. But the gist of it is, a ghostly lady came down from the sky and pulled the life's spirit out of Jace just like she was pulling goose down out of a pillow. And while the lady was doing it... God, the scream.

She screamed, oh how she screamed. Something awful. Just awful. That banshee wail, just like you heard about when you was a kid only a hundred times worse. A scream like nobody ever heard before and most probably never will hear, if they're lucky. A scream like a thousand lambs being led to slaughter. A scream to torment the living, a scream to lift the dead and carry them the rest of the way on to hell.

"I won't ever get that scream out of my mind, Teddy," Brandy would say in the coming years, when she worked up enough strength to talk about it again. "Not if I live to be eighty years old. Not if I live to be a hundred, not if I live forever. Not ever."

Uncle Ted paused his story. He looked down at the loose pile of playing cards on the tabletop in front him, flipped his finger back and forth through them. It was plain to all of us that he hadn't forgotten the scream he heard that night, either.

"It was the Boone Creek Banshee, come down to carry Jace Watkins away," he finally whispered to the suddenly-quiet roomful of partygoers. "Just like she'd carried away every other man in his family. His granddad, his dad, his brother. She got 'em all, and then she got poor Jace to boot. The damnedest thing I ever saw. I wouldn't have believed it if I didn't see it myself."

I got brave and decided to ask a question. Even at that young age I was already a pretty good student of folklore, and something about the story just didn't sit right with me.

"I thought banshees were only in Ireland?" I asked.

My uncle raised an eyebrow at my question. "You read that in one of your books, Grady?"

"Mmmm-hmmm."

He looked around the room, making eye contact with everyone. "I've heard that, too. But I'm telling you, this was a banshee. There's not a doubt in my mind. Ain't nothing else that could make such a terrible sound. Ain't nothing else fits Brandy's description. Maybe it's all the damn Irishman that come over in the old days. Germans and English and Irish, that's all they had up in the hills. All I can tell you, it was a by-hell banshee, and it got Jace, and I'm pretty damn sure that we ain't in Ireland."

"He's telling the truth, too. Banshees are real," I heard a familiar voice say from the far corner. "Real as anybody in this room. And Jace Watkins ain't the first person that she took from this part of the country, either. Uh uh. This one's been around for a while."

When those words were spoken, everybody turned together to see Jasper Bohanon standing behind us all, arms folded across his chest. He'd been there for a good while, I supposed – at least long enough to hear that whole story about Jace and the banshee – but somehow I hadn't seen him until now. Actually this was the first time I'd seen him since the end of school. It looked like he'd grown an inch in that time.

"What do you know about it?" I asked, not intending it hateful even though I could tell that he took it that way. I was just curious, that's all.

Jasper looked right at me. "I saw her myself," he said. "I saw her and I'm still here to talk about it. That's what I know."

Now, we weren't sure what to think. Not one bit. I'd played with enough of his G.I. Joes and read through enough of his *Fangoria* magazines to feel safe in saying that I knew him better than anybody else in that concrete-block building, but I'd never heard him mention any such encounter. Still, the way he said he'd seen that banshee, the way he sounded so sure of himself, I didn't have a good reason to doubt it.

After Jasper said his piece, Uncle Teddy gave him a long look.

"You're one of Grady's friends, ain't ya?" he said.

"Yes, sir," said Jasper.

"How about that." Teddy bit his lip, pondered on it some more. "So you saw the banshee too, huh?"

"Yes, sir."

"When?"

"I saw her twice, actually," said Jasper. He stepped out of the corner. I swear, the adults parted to let him through to our card table.

"Hey Boo," he said to me quietly when he got there.

"Hey Jasper," I said back. I have to admit, I felt a certain pride at that moment.

Uncle Teddy stood up straight.

"Twice? You mean to tell that you – what are you, twelve years old? – that *you* saw the Boone Creek banshee not once, but twice?"

Jasper didn't flinch. "That's exactly what I mean to tell," he said. "And there's something else, too."

"What's that?"

"I know where she's at. I know where she's at *right now*."

Uncle Ted's face took on a serious look. "You wouldn't come in here and bullshit a bunch of grown-ups, would you kid?"

"Nope. I mean I know where you can find that banshee, if you want," Jasper repeated. "And if you'll drive, I can take you there."

Fifteen minutes later, we headed out to Boone Creek. Me, Jasper, Uncle Ted, and his dogs, all piled together on the front bench seat of a '74 Chevy pick-up.

BANSHEE

On the way, Teddy and Jasper talked about the banshee, batting questions back and forth, each one trying to get a feel for whether the other was telling the truth or full of horseshit. How's she look? What sort of dress does she wear? What's she sound like? It was the most intense conversation I ever heard between a grown man and a kid not quite in sixth grade

I'd been considering this whole banshee scenario and have to admit, up to that point my doubts far outweighed any belief I had that we'd be seeing anything supernatural that night. Figured it was just another ghost story that the grown-ups told to make each other laugh when they were all good and soused.

But as Jasper and Teddy kicked the notion back and forth, I started to believe. I tried not to believe – sure I did – but the way they talked about it, the way they bought into every word they said just like it was pulled straight out of the King James, *the way their stories matched down to the last detail,* I couldn't help but think that maybe this wasn't some old ghost story, after all. They could have been pulling my chain, of course. I thought about that possibility, I swear I did. But the whole time, they just kept passing details to one another, going a little deeper into their stories with each comment. Never cracked one smile between them, either, Serious business.

Trust me when I say that if you'd have been there you'd have come to the same conclusion I did: they were telling the truth. At the very least, they *believed* they were telling the truth, and as I've come to learn, belief is all it takes to give breath to the most fantastic of ideas.

After a few minutes we turned off the highway and onto a gravel service road, winding through the tall weeds towards the bank of Boone Creek. Finally we came to rest near a wide, still part of the creek that probably was used for a swimming hole by the local farm kids and also for a pissing spot by the cows in the surrounding pastures.

Across the creek, the land curled back and in just a few yards turned into a hillside that was thick with briar bushes and spindly old maple trees. The full moon shone clear enough that we could see pretty much whatever we needed, at least from the creek back through the field.

Up the hillside, it was a little different. The summer leaves blocked out enough of the moonbeams that the hill wasn't much more than a black tangle of tree limbs and wicked underbrush. If we walked that way, it'd be hard to see more than eight or ten feet in one direction, even with a flashlight. I can't say I looked forward to stumbling around out there blind, especially given the reason we'd come out here.

Uncle Teddy popped the truck into park, switched off the engine and the headlights, and jumped out. "Here Homer. Here Henry," he whispered, and his two dogs jumped right after him. The dogs were leashed but when they hit the ground, they each took a couple of steps then stopped still around Teddy's feet. Kept their noses up, pointed towards the woods, twitching.

They whined a little bit, turned a couple circles then pointed back in the same direction of the trees. I took it as they wasn't scared in the slightest, just raring to get after it. But I could have been wrong.

Me and Jasper followed them out of the truck. As soon as I shut the door behind me, Teddy asked, "You boys don't get too far away from me now. Your mothers will have my ass if I lose you. Which way y'all going?"

"Over there," Jasper answered. He pointed up the creek towards a little limestone overhang, where the water had receded enough to leave a spit of gravel wide enough for us to walk across. "She likes to hang out over there, past that rock and back into the woods a little piece."

"You don't know that," said Teddy. "She could be anywhere. Me and Jace ran into her a quarter mile thataway." He motioned down the creek in the opposite direction.

"Nah, she's up there." Jasper took off walking and I went with him.

"Do what you want," Teddy said. "I'm takin' the dogs and we're going out there. First one sees anything, give a big holler so we can all hear, got it?"

Jasper didn't break stride. "I got it."

*

We walked around for an hour or so, across that gravel spit, up the bank and back into the woods, but never did see the Boone Creek Banshee. The night stayed silent, more or less. Every now and again we'd hear Homer or Henry crash through the thickets further down the darkened hillside, but then they'd get clear and everything would turn quiet again and you could hear your own breath sink down into the bottom of your chest.

It wasn't long before boredom settled in. Maybe Jasper and Uncle Teddy had actually seen the banshee, maybe they hadn't. I was still willing to offer the benefit of the doubt, but regardless of whether they had or not, it was starting to look like nobody would be seeing her that night at all.

I mentioned to Jasper that we should meet Ted back at the truck, and after a little bit of discussion, he agreed, even though I could tell he didn't want to. We turned around, retracing our footsteps back to the creek.

"Maybe we can come back some other time," I said.

"We will." He gazed into the trees. "She's out here, Boo. She's out here somewhere, sure as all get out. That banshee's real, you can count on that, and if we don't find her tonight we'll find her another night."

He took a deep breath. Thinking.

As I was formulating a proper response, I looked up and saw her.

The banshee.

Jasper did, too, the same time that I did.

"Holy shit! Right there!" He pointed back into the woods, at a bluish white glow that floated a few feet above the ground. It was the Boone Creek banshee. No other thought crossed my mind. It was her, sure as anything and everything, just like Jasper said.

My mouth went dry. My throat tightened up just like I'd swallowed a spoonful of salt.

I took off running.

"Where you going?" Jasper called after me, but I didn't answer and he didn't say anything else, neither. I didn't *have* to say anything else, because a half-second later his footsteps were bearing down right behind me. Together we ran, and we didn't stop running until we got to creek's edge, jumped over the bank and took a five foot drop onto wet gravel. There, we put our backs against the limestone, and we waited.

I felt my breath getting heavy in my lungs, waiting for that banshee to come find us. My blood pounded in my ears; I clenched my teeth so hard that I could feel cracks forming in the porcelain crowns. Jasper didn't look any better, neither. What we thought was such a great idea just a few minutes before – stomping around out here, looking for the supernatural – now felt like the foolish want of ignorant minds. But then, staring death in the face can change a lot of perceptions.

Me and Jasper stood still underneath that mossy overhang for a few seconds. It could have been longer, a minute or two, hell, maybe an hour. I lost track of all time. The only reality was the air caught in my throat, the hot blood that throbbed in my ears and behind my eyes. At some point in the night, though, a white glow descended over the edge of the bank and started moving out over the water, and right behind that glow – above it, actually – materialized the banshee of Boone Creek.

The banshee floated above our heads, to the edge of the creek bank, then over us, then beyond us. We watched her hover across the water, suspended in mid-air with arms out to the sides. Her spectral white dress trailed in the atmosphere, long enough that I thought I might be able to reach it from where I stood.

I held back, though, even as she moved away from us. I didn't want to take any chances; I'd seen the banshee, enough to suit me just fine.

Jasper felt differently. He stepped away from the limestone wall and went past me, a quiet stride into the creek with one hand outstretched, reaching for her.

I moved to pull him back, but she never turned around. The thumping in my ears slowed as I realized this spirit from a world beyond had no concern for two curious boys in the summer before their sixth grade year. Me and Jasper let her go. And go she did, skimming across the creek and the other side of the bank, into the woods beyond. Never got close to the ground, either. Her surrounding white glow lit the way, and I watched that soft light fade back into the trees the same way that on some other summer night I might watch a firefly disappear into the stars.

About the time I thought she was gone for good, Homer and Henry started braying.

They crashed through the underbrush, headed towards us.

"You boys come over here?" Uncle Teddy called. "Grady? Jasper? Can you all hear me now?"

I wanted to answer, tell him to be quiet and not draw unwanted attention, but it was too late. Already, up the hillside, the banshee glow started moving back towards us.

Teddy's hounds spotted the light before he did. They jumped around, yelped and whined and yelped some more, louder and stronger as the spirit come near. Ted scanned the woods in the direction they were looking, and soon enough he saw the same thing they did.

That's when he froze.

I'd never seen anything like it. The image is stamped on my brain forever: Uncle Ted, his back to us, looking up into the trees while he held his dogs fast by the leash, all of them stuck in position just like they was rooted right to the ground, all of them silhouetted against the backlight of that ghostly luminescence – that cold banshee light, as I'd come to call it for the rest of my life – that now eased out of the woods, creeping towards them.

He yelled "Get to the truck, boys!" but all of us knew there wasn't time. We'd never make it.

To make matters worse, that glow was moving faster, already so close that it wasn't just a glow anymore, but the banshee full-formed. I could make out the wisps of her dress, and her thin fingers reaching for us. And the delicate features of her face, too, only they weren't so delicate now, but pulled back hard, and sinister, and angry.

Angry at all of us.

Uncle Teddy realized what was happening at the same time I did. He turned and yanked the leash on his dogs, pulling them towards the truck, which was a good forty yards away. "Get on now! Get on!" he implored the animals, but they just sat there, whining, scared as the rest of us.

The banshee eased down, out of the treetops, into the open. The bottom of her dress skimmed through the night just a few feet from Uncle Teds eye level, or what would have been his eye level if he hadn't been running away.

"Get on now, you bastards!" he cried again, but still those dogs didn't move.

Now, he couldn't wait anymore for them to get going on their own, and gave the leashes one last yank. This time it was enough.

When Homer and Henry felt Teddy tugging at their collars, they lit out like somebody put fire ants in their Puppy Chow, dragging my uncle behind in something like a clumsy dash, stumbling and splashing through the brackish waters. In the bright moonlight I could see his eyes were big as golf balls and about as white, too.

Two steps into the creek, she caught him.

While Ted kicked warm splashes into his own face, the banshee swooped around and came up at his eye level, which put her directly in between him and us. She hovered there, staring him down with her eyes even with his, her hands dangling out front and legs flowing up behind her at an angle, the bottom of her dress resting higher than her head did, like she'd dived down to the bottom of the pool and was reaching for something to take back up with her. Which I guess, in a way, that's exactly what she was doing.

Uncle Ted stopped. That's what he did. Just stopped, and stood straight, and looked at her. I don't know if he was overcome with fear or if he just flat gave up without a fight, but then again I never knew my Uncle Ted to give up on anything.

He let go of his dogs, too. They ran over the truck and hid under it and the lady never paid them any more mind.

Teddy stood there, up to his shins in Boone Creek, with that eerie creature in the air out front of him, her face not ten inches from his.

And then, that banshee started screaming.

I swear, the temperature dropped fifteen degrees in a heartbeat. What had been a muggy summer night now shuddered beneath her terrible wail. That cry had a power you can't imagine and I can't describe except to say that you never heard anything like it, and never will unless you face it on your own.

It was a jagged blade that almost split me and Jasper in half, and it drove Uncle Teddy to his knees. I wanted to help, wanted to run to him, but

Jasper grabbed me by the shoulder and pulled me back before I got too far towards my own doom.

"He's hers, now," my friend whispered. He was right.

The banshee moved in for her final kiss. When she did, me and Jasper jumped up on the bank and took off on a dead run, fast as we could get out of there. We didn't give a thought to the truck, or Homer, or Henry. All we concerned ourselves with was getting as far as we could in the opposite direction of that banshee, in as short a time as we could do it.

Not long after we started running, Uncle Teddy cried out.

I slowed down just enough that I could glance over my shoulder, but there wasn't anything to see. To be honest, when I think about it now, I'm *glad* I couldn't see anything. I whipped my head back around, looked straight forward, and kept going, with Jasper a couple strides ahead of me.

We heard a soft splash as Teddy's body hit the water, then everything got quiet behind us. I didn't look back again until we were halfway home.

I never knew I could run that far without stopping, but right there in that moment I come to learn that under the hairiest of circumstances, pure fear can give a person certain capabilities that they might not otherwise possess. Me and Jasper turned tail and started running the moment that demon woman leaned in on poor Uncle Teddy, and we didn't pull up again until we were a good three miles down the road. And sure as I'm sitting here telling this story, I could have gone another three miles if necessary. Absolutely I could have.

We stood in the middle of highway 213, breathing hard, saturated with sweat, partly because we'd just galloped those three miles and partly because we'd just had the sweet crap scared out of us. I doubled over, hands on knees, taking air in deep draws. Jasper did the same. Neither one of us said anything for a good ten minutes.

I kept looking down the road behind us, waiting for that banshee light to appear, but it never did.

Finally, Jasper said, "We should have known better than to go chasing after that thing."

"Gee, ya think?"

"Yeah." He looked off to one side, nodded his head slowly, blinked a few times. Jasper blinked a lot, whenever he was deep pondering one of his big ideas. "A banshee's supposed to be some kind of a death harbinger."

"A what?"

"A harbinger."

"Yeah. I guess so," I said. "She sure just harbingered Uncle Ted pretty good."

"You never heard that word before?"

I stood up straight. "Course I've heard it. It's like... a sign. An omen. Something's on its way."

"Right. Right," Jasper continued. "It's just like that. A sign of what's coming. Banshees come calling for unfortunate souls who're soon to be leaving this world for the next one. And if those souls ain't quite ready to go, the banshee haunts the grounds anyhow, just waiting until time's up. That's how they're a harbinger – if you see one, you know death ain't far behind. And when the moment comes that it's time for somebody to die, the banshee lets off the god-awfulest scream, like they want the angels up in Heaven to know they're on their way. Or the devils down in Hell. *Here we come, open up the gate 'cause I got a fresh one,* that's what that wail means. Sure enough, that's what it means."

His words trailed off. He looked at me for a second, then turned away.

I wasn't quite sure what I should say. In that moment, my friend had sunk into a dark place, speaking in an icy whisper that crawled across my soul.

Jasper walked a circle, then faced me again. "Hey Boo, there's one other thing."

"What?"

"Did you know that a banshee is tied to a certain family? Follows the men down through the years. Did you know that?"

I shook my head.

"It's true," he said. "Think about it. Jace Watkins was Ted's cousin. She got him. Just like she got Ted. You said all Jace's relatives died in awful ways, the bitch probably got them, too –"

I shook my head. "His daddy. His brother, his grandfather. They just died, nothing unnatural about it. Cancer. War –"

"You really believe that? After what you saw tonight?"

I hesitated.

Of course I didn't believe that.

But –

Jasper took a step towards me. He lowered his voice, like there might be somebody else out there with us on that two-lane country road, somebody listening that he didn't want to hear.

"War. Right. Cancer. Right. Listen up, friend," he said. "Listen up if you know what's good. Those were just stories your Uncle told. He wasn't there when they died. He don't know. One thing I know, the banshee got Jace's granddad, then she got his dad, then she got his brother, then finally she got Jace."

He thought about it some more.

"Jace Watkins. He was your uncle's cousin, right?"

I nodded. "Mmmm-hmmm." Didn't like where this was headed, not one bit.

"Jace was the last of his line. So when that blood dried up, the banshee moved over to the next one. Like I said, a banshee's tied to one family. You said him and Teddy were first cousins right?"

"Yeah. He's my mom's brother. But –"

"Correct me if I'm wrong, but that means you got the same bloodlines, don't it? How about your grandfather, your mom's dad? How did he die?"

"He... he had a car wreck. It happened before I was born."

"A car wreck," Jasper repeated. "A car wreck, before you were born. How about that."

I knew what he was getting at, but didn't want to think about it anymore. Not tonight. Blood thumped in my ears again and soon Jasper's words turned to unintelligible drone before eventually they just died out completely.

We started walking, and by the time we got home, the sun peeked over the hilltop. The Boone Creek banshee didn't show herself again that next night, or the one after. I'd love to tell you she stayed away from us forever, too – that she disappeared from Whistle Mill that night and never bothered our family again. Oh, how I would surely love telling you that. Alas…

INFINITY

Me and Jasper went back to Boone Creek the next morning, figuring we would gather Uncle Teddy's body and tell everybody he'd got lit up on Jack Daniels whiskey, that he fell face-first in a swimming hole and drowned before we could get to him. We didn't know if anybody would actually *believe* that story, but in the end we never told it, anyway.

When we got back to the creek, we found Uncle Ted's body downstream a hundred yards or so, lapping up against the bank, caught amongst a briar tangle. His skin and hair were turned the same bright white color, or to be more exact, non-color. His eyes were wide and blank, his mouth frozen open, as if he'd died screaming and carried that scream right on with him into the afterlife. I suppose that's exactly what happened, too.

Ted's truck rested right where he left it. Homer and Henry had laid underneath the back end, and were crying something awful when we saw them. I guessed they got spooked as bad as the rest of us. After a moment's discussion we decided that the only proper course of action was one, keeping those dogs, and two, keeping our mouths shut about our encounter with the banshee.

With that settled, I scooped up Homer, while Jasper took Henry. Then we spit on the ground, swore not to tell anybody else about what we'd seen that night, and headed home.

The summer moved on. Life moved on. The universe moved on.

Sheriff Slone and his boys came out and got Uncle Ted's body. We had the funeral three days later. Uncle Ted's death was a news story for a little while – "WHISTLE MILL MAN DROWNS IN BOONE CREEK" – but eventually the news moved on, too. (He never had a wife or kids, which meant my mom and I were the only family he had left when he died.) My parents tried talking with me about what had happened, but there wasn't much I could say. Not much I could say to them, anyway.

I'd lay awake some nights, wondering if I might look up and see that banshee floating outside my window, waiting for me like she waited for so many other men of my relation, but she never came calling. I guess it wasn't my time yet.

But that was just some nights. Other nights, visions of an entirely different specter kept me from the comfort of sleep. I'd toss and turn, haunted by the image of a ghost hovering just beyond the window glass, peering in at me with dead, unblinking eyeballs. Only those nights, it wasn't the banshee of Boone Creek, it was someone much closer. It was Uncle Ted, one hand scratching at the glass, the other beckoning me to come outside and join him. Looking at me not with his devilish grin, but instead with an accusatory expression. And while his lips never moved, I could still hear his voice in my head.

Why'd you let her take me, Grady?

I thought we was family.

Why?

Why?

Why?

I couldn't answer.

Teddy's death chewed at the edges of my soul. That's all there was to it. I couldn't have done anything to stop it, I knew that, but still those memories gnawed on me like rats gnawing on a wire cage. Sometimes I could squeeze my eyelids shut and when I opened them back up, the rats would be gone, everything would be gone. Sometimes. But not every time.

Along the way, Mom got the sense I was carrying a new burden. She'd ask what was bothering me – she asked me that often – but I'd always drop my gaze towards my chest and say, "Nothing."

Mom and Dad never pushed it much more than that, but I could tell she never believed me. They may not have known exactly *what* was going on, but still, they knew something was eating away at me. Mom even bought me a subscription to *Fangoria* in the hope it might ease some of my troubles. And truth be told, it did help.

I doubt my parents ever felt convinced I was doing okay then, but I wasn't all that interested in setting their minds at ease. It's not that I didn't care what they thought – they were my Mom and

Dad, of course I cared what they thought – but the way I looked at it, they were parents and as parents, it was their job to worry and there wasn't a thing on Earth could change that. Guess I just figured they'd keep asking "Are you all right?" while days kept coming off the calendar ad the seasons kept ticking by us, until eventually we'd all just sort of move along to something else.

We did, too. At least, they did. I kept my mind on the banshee, and anything else like her that might be out there, lurking in the woods around Whistle Mill.

Looking back on it, I probably didn't do as good a job as I thought, trying to hide the mysteries that afflicted my juvenile brain now that I knew beyond any doubt there was a whole new fantastic world out there waiting for me. The Boone Creek banshee was behind door number one. I knew that there were a lot more doors to be opened.

I pondered on it a lot.

During the coming months, me and Jasper kept the Boone Creek Banshee to ourselves. We never talked about it in the presence of anyone else, figuring that was for the best. Who'd believe that story, anyway? We already felt like we were outside, looking in. No need to make it even worse on ourselves.

When the summer burned off the calendar, classes kicked back into gear. I started sixth grade at Seward County Middle School. It was the first year that I had to rotate classrooms and teachers with each subject. It was also the first year without recess, which meant no more G.I. Joe swaps during school hours.

Fortunately, Jasper was in my homeroom, which meant we were together all day, going from class to class. If you ever went to middle school you know it's an awful bitter spoonful to choke down even on the best days. We might not have had recess but we still shared *Fangoria*s; we just had to be a little more discrete about it, passing the magazines back and forth during class when the teachers weren't looking.

It's a fair statement that middle school happened in our lives with as much excitement as a fart in a Halloween mask. "The miasma of mediocrity," that's how Jasper referred to our surroundings (I had to look up "miasma" when he first used that phrase), and that bad smell clung to us hard. In our clothes, our hair, our eyes, everywhere. We couldn't get away from it and I'd be lying if I didn't admit there was plenty of days when I thought we'd *never* shake the smell out.

I'd look at the other kids at school and just feel sorry for the lot of them. Sorry for all the truth they didn't know, sorry for all the truth they didn't even *want* to know. Me and Jasper had crossed paths with a mythical creature; what had those other kids done? While they were worried about basketball and who they could take to the May Dance, me and Jasper never had time for that. Instead we spent our days and nights thinking about what might be in the darkness, ready to yank us down by the shoulders when we weren't looking. Or even when we *were* looking.

So, our classmates went on with their happy, unaware lives, but meanwhile we spent ours hip-deep in scary movies, monster books, and *Fangoria* magazine. Fortunately for us, in the few months after the episode with Uncle Ted and the Boone Creek banshee, no other supernatural buggers reared their head in that part of the world, which left plenty of time for educating ourselves in the how-tos and what-fors of the horror world.

We dove in headlong, too. The 1980s were heady days for the horror genre, with an explosion of material unlike anything known before. Me and Jasper took full advantage. I spent a lot of time at the local public library, reading books both fiction and not, writing down their titles in case Jasper might not have read them yet, which as it turned out wasn't very often.

Not just books about ghosts and creatures from the real world, either, although I did read a shit-ton of those. I also blew through all the best horror writers of the era, guys like Stephen King (*Salem's Lot, It, The Stand, Cycle of the Werewolf*), Clive Barker (*Books of Blood*), Joe Lansdale (*The Drive-in*), John Skipp and Craig Spector (*The Light at the End, The Cleanup*), Robert McCammon (*Swan Song*), and Dan Simmons (*Song of Kali, Carrion Comfort*). In those days you couldn't walk ten feet through a Walgreen's or Piggly Wiggly without running into a carousel loaded down with paperback books, and most of those paperbacks were of the scare genre.

It was a golden age of horror novels and me and Jasper lapped up every bit of it. If nothing else the books kept my imagination active, which was everything when dealing with the fantastic world. You had to keep your mind flexed. Couldn't let your guard drop.

As much as I got into it, though, Jasper went that much deeper. Weeks would go by where I'd never see him outside of school, and even in school he'd barely look up from his reading material long enough to say hey. When he finally did come back around he'd start spouting off stories and facts that even I hadn't come across in all my studies, about some Scandinavian wind demon or Mexican vampire or Native American soul stealer. Then that discussion would lurch off into another one about whether or not we could handle something like that if it ever showed up on our front porch. Which, even back then, we always felt pretty good that we could handle whatever come our way. Even if we weren't even teenagers yet.

Besides the monster talk, we also took to philosophizing. Now we knew there was more to the world than what most people saw, and that gave us all the more reason to let our minds wander in certain theoretical directions, trying to make sense of everything around us. The universe kept expanding, getting bigger with every minute that passed in our lives. This fact couldn't go unnoticed by two boys with plenty of time on their hands.

One of Jasper's favorite topics was infinity. It started as just a concept in math class, a point in the distance that you could ponder over but never feel that you understood, but before long it became such a part of our ongoing conversations that I began to sense he was taking it on as part of his personal worldview.

"There's something out there," he liked to say, motioning towards the sky. He usually brought it up at night, when he could point into the deep, never ending black void above us.

"What do you think it is?" I'd ask, or at least a certain variation of that. I couldn't claim to know the answer but I did have a curiosity about it.

"I can't tell you exactly what, Boo. But it's something. Something, you bet your backside. There's too much out there to be full of a whole lot of nothing, that's the way I look at it. Too much, just too damn much."

"The thing about infinity," he would always say, "is that a lot of people think of it as a number. But it's not a number, you know? It's beyond numbers. It's beyond human reason. Hell, there's people can't come to grips with dinosaurs being real, cause there ain't nothing around these days that's comparable. Like there ain't no pterodactyls flying around, so that must mean they never existed.

"Those are people that can't get their hands around just how long sixty million years really is. And sixty million years, that's just a whisper on the timeline of the universe, so sayin' dinosaurs can't be real because they ain't around no more is like sayin' you're blinded for life because you blinked on the day you were born. Never mind how much the world's changed just in the last hundred."

I would always nod my head. Truth be told, I never gave it that much thought. I just agreed with my friend for the sake of agreement. Jasper was the philosopher among us; I was content to indulge him, but for me, once the conversation ended, the metaphysical questions disappeared, like so many campfire embers disappearing in smoky air. They never disappeared for Jasper.

"Infinity ain't a point on a line," he'd say. "It's *every* point on *every* line. It's possibility, that's what it is. Naw, hell, it's more than that. It's *all* possibilities. You hear, Boo? Most folks know that if you played the lottery every day for an infinite number of days, eventually you'll hit. The math's pretty easy. It's just combinations. You got a finite number of combinations and an infinite number of chances, eventually you'll get there.

"But what people don't think about is, if you play the lottery for an infinite amount of time, eventually, you'll hit the numbers not just once, but ten times. A hundred times. A thousand times. Think about it: if you play the lottery across infinity, at some point you'll hit the Powerball a billion times in a row. *A billion times in a row.*"

This was usually the point where I started to get a little fuzzy with the numbers. But he wouldn't stop.

"It's long odds. You bet it is. A few million trillion quintillion to one. Hell, it's probably worse than that if you actually sit down and do the math. What are the exact odds of hitting the Powerball numbers a billion times in a row? That's why they got math teachers, I guess.

"But whatever it is, I can tell you this: you got a certain set of numbers and a certain set of combinations. That means you can only get so many outcomes. Your odds ain't ever zero. You play forever and eventually you'll hit everything. Then you'll hit everything again. And then you'll just keep going. And keep going. And keep going.

"That's infinity. Possibilities. It's all things, without an end. It's space, not time or numbers. It's the point when everything that *could* happen, *has* happened; it's not about how long it might take for shit to happen, it's knowing that shit *will* happen. Guaranteed. Everything that ever was, everything that will be, and everything that ever could be. You get me?"

I didn't. Well, I sort of did. More than anything, I figured we would talk about this a lot in the years to come. In the meantime, we had middle school to get through, which as any seventh grader will tell you, is pretty much Hell on Earth.

Actually, any seventh grader will tell you that middle school is worse than Hell on Earth.

PART TWO

MIDDLE SCHOOL
AND
OTHER HORRORS

ETHEL MARIE STANTON

That's no overstatement, saying that middle school is worse Hell on Earth. All those boys and girls with more hairspray than brains, hormones waging holy war on the inside, their bodies waging holy war against each other on the outside. Makes for quite a circus freak show. If you went through it – and I'm guessing you did – then you know what I mean.

It's like for some reason, God sat down one afternoon and decided he needed to come up with the perfect torture device for little boys, something to crack their bones on both ends and slice their hearts clean down the middle, and after about five seconds thought, the Almighty came up with grades six through eight. Something akin to boot camp – survive without getting your ass kicked too many times, and they'll let you gear up and move on to high school. The big leagues.

The truth is, middle school is no place for outsiders, and when you love *Fangoria* and horror movies and comic books, you're an outsider with a capital O. That's just how it is. While the rest of the kids went about their days playing grab-ass in the hallways, talking about basketball and whatever was on TV the night before, me and Jasper mostly kept to ourselves. While all the other kids past love notes and went to holiday dances, my friend and I stood against the wall and let the crowds pass us by. I think that's what kept us sane. Not only did we not understand them, we didn't *want* to understand them. We stayed away.

That part of this story is just your average cool kids-versus-nerds story. You've seen it a million times and I don't feel all that compelled to hash it out again. At least now you know where we fit in the lay of the land. Of course you also know we were the only two kids in Seward County to face down a banshee and live to talk about it, so there's that.

One other thing that sticks in my mind about me and Jasper's middle school days – besides the general abundance of hairspray and neon bracelets of the era – is that for some reason, a lot of grown-ups around Whistle Mill were convinced that a shadowy band of Satanists roamed the countryside, picking off little kids and sacrificing them to the Dark Lord. These Satanists were said to particularly favor children with blonde hair and blue eyes, which meant that not only were they a bunch of devil worshippers, they were apparently Nazis to boot. (The Nazi link didn't occur to me until several years later.) So, whenever a big community gathering like the Orchid Festival or the Whistle Mill Ice Cream Social or the Seward County Fair would come up, these frightened parents would lock up their kids for the night, especially if the little ones were blessed with the Satanists' preferred appearance.

Me and Jasper had barely hit our teenage years at that point, but even then, this widespread fear of bloody Satanic rituals didn't make a whole hell of a lot of sense. Not from where we stood, anyway. Why would a band of Satanists set up camp in little ol' Whistle Mill, Kentucky? If they were looking for sacrifices, wouldn't they have more to pick from in, say, a larger city like Lexington or Louisville? In a town with just a few hundred children, not all of which had blonde hair and blue eyes anyway, it seemed like the sacrificial options would run out pretty quickly. Then what? Would the Satanists simply move on to the next town and pick up where they left off? Or would Satan himself accept brunettes as a matter of appeasement, if brunettes were all his minions could offer? Who knew.

Now I'm not saying any of this was supposed to make any rational sense. All I'm sayin is, it's what folks believed at the time. One thing I know about this world, sometimes being rational ain't necessarily at the top of everyone's to-do list, and it's not at the top of many lists at all in insulated little towns like Whistle Mill. People believe what they want to believe no matter how whacked out their ideas might seem to others. It's more comfortable that way. And the harder you try to shake some sense into them, the harder they hold on to that comfort. That's the one truth that ain't never changed in all the years that humans have been walking this Earth. Probably never will.

Then again, we *are* talking about a time when Ronald Wilson Reagan was president of the U.S.

of A., so I can see how certain segments of the country might have felt there were dark forces aligned against them.

Leading our community's charge against dat ole mean debbil was a pious old lady by the name of Ethel Marie Stanton. She'd been the librarian at Seward County Middle School since before the war, and which war that was, nobody around was old enough to remember for sure. She was a short little hamster-faced woman, with wire eyeglasses and a poofed up salt-and-pepper hairdo that sat perched atop her righteous skull like a sleepy raccoon, cemented in place by enough hairspray to lacquer a gymnasium floor.

Me and Jasper never did get along too great with Ms. Stanton. There were a few different reasons, but mostly they came down to the fact that she just didn't see the world the same way we did. She saw Satan everywhere, an all-threatening evil that could only be overcome through school sponsored prayer groups and pithy Bible verses fired rat-a-tat-tat like they were coming hot out of a Gatling gun. We preferred to take more of a broader view.

Now, if Ethel Stanton had kept her business to herself, if she'd just stuck with her Bible verses and prayer groups, everything would have been fine. She'd have stayed out of our way and we'd have stayed out of hers.

But of course, she couldn't do that.

In her mind, she had to save us from ourselves. Like how she launched a campaign and got all the Stephen King books pulled from every library in the county, even though she'd never read one in her life.

Like how she showed up every Friday at our local video store to rant at any customers who might be perusing the horror section.

Like how she got not just *Fangoria* banned from the schools, but movie magazines in general. Comic books, too.

Like how she told my parents and Jasper's at a parent teacher conference that she feared that our interest in horror movies could lead down the road to us becoming full-blown serial killers.

She did. She said that. Ethel Stanton told our parents that she feared me and Jasper might become serial killers. I wasn't there but Mom and Dad weren't exactly thrilled about it, and it was a major topic of conversation between them when they got back home later that evening. And believe me, sitting here telling you the story, I know just how laughable it sounds. But there may not be a better window into the way her brain worked.

Still, as much as she aggravated us and as much as we thought she was about three cards short of a half-assed poker hand, we figured it was best to just stay the hell away from her. Her antics weren't anything more than the ravings of a backwards old lady with too much time on her hands. In the life of a little boy it can be a pretty big deal when the lunatic school librarian takes your Stephen King books and your *Fangoria* magazines and your Marvel comics and swears to the world that they're all Satan's rags, not fit to wipe the dingle berries from the hind end of a dog. But in the grand scheme of the infinite universe, Ms. Ethel Marie Stanton was about as relevant as a fart in a hurricane, no matter what she thought otherwise. She could take our books and comics out of the school. We'd just get more.

Unfortunately when it comes to people like Ethel Marie Stanton, you can't just stay out of their way – they tend to make a point of getting in yours all too often. It's not enough for them to cherish their beliefs; they think *everybody* ought to cherish the same beliefs they do. I'd call it a funny way of looking at freedom of religion – we're all free to think what we want, unless we slip up and start thinking differently from them.

It's safe to say, despite mine and Jasper's best efforts, we still had our run-ins with ol' Ethel. With as stupid as we thought she was, and as lost as she thought we were, I suppose a little head-butting was bound to happen. Her saying we'd grow up to be mass murderers didn't help anything.

Eventually, it all came to a head.

The end actually began at the Movie Place.

Before I get into all of this, let me explain the importance of VHS videotape during my formative years. As I've made plain, me and Jasper watched a ton of movies, considered them crucial to our raising. And most of those movies, we saw on VHS. The other options were limited, locally speaking.

The only theater in the county was a drive-in in Sewardville, the Mountain View Drive-in Theater. We'd get out there a few times a year for a double-bill of new releases, especially if they were playing on the main screen. (The second screen was mostly the domain of lesser films, Burt Reynolds and Rodney Dangerfield vehicles that didn't do much for us at all.) Suck down a couple buckets of hot buttered popcorn, a gallon of Coca-Cola each, maybe even a pepperoni and sausage pizza if we were extra hungry.

As far as TV, cable and satellite weren't widespread in those days, but we'd catch whatever science fiction film happened across the networks. Mostly *Star Wars* and *Star Trek,* or the occasional kid flick like *The Neverending Story* or *The Dark Crystal.* In the early eighties, ABC showed a few horror movies as part of their "Sunday Night Movie," series – that was the first place I ever saw *Alligator, Jaws 2,* and *Alien* – but by the end of the decade, the only place you could find any horror was after midnight on the local channels, where they'd show scary movies just because they figured the only people watching that late were those looking for a little bit of a creep up the back of their necks. I saw *Friday the 13th Part 3* and *Wolfen* that way, along with some obscure Italian zombie movies.

But for the most part, our movie viewing took place via the magic of half-inch VHS tape.

Being that this was the 1980s, video rental stores were at the unquestioned apex of their Golden Age. Seemed like when Mom took me to

Lexington, you couldn't travel a half mile without passing one, with its windows full of fading movie posters that were framed by light bulbs in a particular way meant to remind folks of movie theater displays, even though it always seemed to me that they never looked like anything other than video store displays. I gave them credit for trying, though.

Our little town of Whistle Mill might not have had much, but in those days, through some manner of odd magic, we somehow were blessed with two video rental stores to call our own.

One of the stores was actually just a small section in the front of the I.G.A., next to the cigarette counter. The pickings were slim there, but at least they had one copy each of all the new releases and a few holdover action movies that maintained popularity with the local clientele. (Chuck Norris movies were particular favorites. *Invasion U.S.A., Code of Silence, Good Guys Wear Black, Missing in Action* and the like.) I couldn't put up much of a fight if you allowed that wasn't a real store, just a few shelves with movie boxes stacked on them. But at least it was something.

That being said, the I.G.A.'s best efforts were no match for the Movie Place.

The Movie Place, indeed. Folks who concerned themselves with such important topics universally agreed that in Whistle Mill, Kentucky the Movie Place was *the* store in town for video rentals. Let me tell you what, that little shop was bona fide – they may not have had the same light-up poster frames as the bigger, fancier stores up in Lexington, but they had more than enough legit movie goods to make up for it. At the Movie Place, they loved the product as much as the customers did. You could tell that as soon as you walked through the door.

Fresh popcorn steamed in a glass case on the front counter. If you wanted, you could get a handful and watch a few minutes of whatever was playing on the nearby big-screen TV. Indiana Jones, *Star Wars, Conan the Barbarian*.

The walls were real wood, and the drywall ceiling sloped down at the sides to just a couple feet above an average heighted human's head. The lack of overhead space lent the room a boxed-in sort of feeling that some people might have found uncomfortable, but I loved. Movie posters covered every square inch of wall and ceiling from the baseboards to the room's apex. The triple threat aromas of popcorn butter, poster paper, and treated wood lingered together in the nostrils, welcome and sweet.

The store's owner – a slight, good humored man named Bobby – was smart about how he arranged their posters in a way that reflected the movie sections underneath. NEW RELEASES and DRAMA up front, COMEDY in the middle of the store, all the way back to ACTION and SCIENCE FICTION and HORROR. (These last three sections were the three ones where I mostly stayed on my visits.) Some of the posters overlapped, but not so much that one title obscured any other; all were treated with respect. I appreciated that. A lot of video stores slung their posters on the wall like dirty towels, not caring where they landed or what happened to them after they got there. Not the Movie Place – every one of theirs was free of rips and wrinkles, and perfectly flat as if ironed like a dress shirt on Easter Sunday. I'm telling you, those posters were so clean you could admire your bangs in their paper reflections if you wanted, and I saw more than one middle school-aged girl doing just that.

I found it interesting, too, how legitimate cinema classics rubbed elbows with the decidedly less legitimate and less classic direct-to-video cheesefests that dominated shops of the era. *Alien, The Empire Strikes Back* and *Star Trek II: The Wrath of Khan* hung adjacent to *Trancers* and *Metalstorm: The Destruction of Jared-Syn* in SCIENCE FICTION, while a few feet down the wall in HORROR, one-sheets for *The Exorcist* and *Rosemary's Baby* and *Black Sunday* shared space with displays for *Aliens Deadly Spawn, Blood Beach,* and *The Dorm that Dripped Blood.*

Every weekend, I walked those wine-colored industrial carpet aisles, searching for VHS magic among row after row of video boxes. I was such a regular that I memorized the order of the titles on the shelves from the front door to the far corner. If they dropped a new one in, I simply slid it into my mental catalog and went on. If they got rid of one title or another... actually, it seemed like they never got rid of anything. Another reason I loved the Movie Place.

Most Friday nights, Mom would take me down there, in the days before me and Jasper could drive ourselves. I rarely had to ask – it just got to the point where she penciled it in as a regularly scheduled stop.

We'd arrive and Bobby (I didn't know his last name then and still don't to this day) would have two or three movies waiting at the front counter. He'd pick them from his latest arrivals, knowing the type of movies that I preferred. Usually, he picked well; I'd take his selections off the counter, then start my tour through the shelves and add a couple more. Then we'd head home, I'd watch them all night, and come back the following Saturday for more.

That Friday night – the night that I started along a path to almost being murdered – started out like any other Friday night. Me and Jasper planned to drop by the Seward County Fair the next day for a few spins on what we felt must be the world's most rickety – and thus exciting – carnie rides: the Tilt-a-Whirl, the Scrambler, and the Kick Booty. He'd stay at my house, we'd take in a few horror movies, then go to the Fair the next morning before the lines got too long.

On our way to pick up Jasper, Mom stopped at the Movie Place. Bobby had the usual stack of new movies waiting. But as I stepped forward to take them off his hands, I noticed something didn't seem right. Bobby looked a little green around the gills.

Before I could say anything myself, Mom asked, "Something wrong, Bobby?"

He nodded, slowly. His mouth soon opened into a broad beam that turned his eyes into playful slits. His thin, friendly face was topped off by a thick mop of prematurely gray hair but that impish grin made him look always young. I'd seen that sunny expression a lot, including times when even as a kid I knew it was covering a snide comment about something Bobby didn't feel like bringing out into the open. This was one of those times, though I didn't yet know what had set the torch to his Friday evening.

Mom raised an eyebrow, not sure what was going on, either. Rather than say another word, he motioned towards the HORROR area, where a shriveled old woman was standing underneath a poster for *Friday the 13th: The Final Chapter*, the one showing Jason's hockey mask laying in a pool of blood, with a knife jabbed through one of the eyeholes.

I recognized the lady's drawn-in hamster face immediately. It was Ethel Stanton, the middle school librarian. She had to be seventy-five years old if she was twenty, and there she was, standing in the HORROR section with her eyes closed, silent. She had one arm raised over head just as far as she could raise it. In that high hand she held a book. And I could make out that book clear enough, even from twenty-five feet away. It was a Bible.

A Bible, all right.

I'll give her credit for one thing: she wielded that Bible with the fervent conviction of a true believer. That black King James rested above her head like a mighty talisman, like she was a wizard lighting a righteous signal fire amidst the blackness of some infernal heathen land. I'd had enough run-ins with her at the middle school to know that she thought of herself pretty much the same way, too. The way she saw it, most of the people of Whistle Mill were wayward mules, and she had just the mighty whip to crack us back into the plowline.

The way I saw it, she was a borderline mental patient. But that's neither here nor there. Not yet, anyway.

Mom watched Ms. Stanton for a couple seconds, but nothing happened. The old librarian just stood there, holding that good book aloft, keeping her eyes closed, saying nothing. With her free hand, she stabbed a bony finger in my direction, like that finger was a magic wand and she was casting lightning bolts at demons.

I thought I heard a faint tune in the room, as though she was humming a little hymn to herself, but I wasn't for certain. It could have been the TV.

"Is that Ethel Stanton?" Mom asked Bobby.

"Yeah, he said. "It sure is."

"What's she doing back there?"

He just smiled.

"Is that... has she got a Bible?"

He just smiled.

"Oh-KAY then," Mom said. I felt her hand on my shoulder, gently pulling me in the direction of the exit. "I think we ought to come back another time, Grady –"

I stepped forward, away from Mom's grip. She snapped for me to come back but I acted like

I didn't hear and kept right on going. Friday night was my night to get movies and nothing was gonna keep me from that. Least of all, Ethel Marie Stanton

I eased towards the HORROR section. Before I could get too far, Ms. Stanton opened her eyes, lowered her Bible enough that she could point it squarely in my direction, and said, "I should have *known* you'd come here for this filth, young man!"

That stopped me cold.

"Grady Strange Claremont, you got a soul that needs to be saved. And *you* –"

She pointed her book straight at my Mom.

"You! I can't believe you bring a child into this smut house. Look around! These walls are covered with smut! All this smut on a child's mind, it'll turn him to the devil, I tell you what! *The devil!*"

I heard Mom let out a sharp gasp and thought for sure she was going after the crazy woman. Before she could make a move, Bobby rushed around from behind the counter and headed towards Ms. Stanton himself.

"All right. That's enough, Ethel," he snapped. His impish grin was gone now. "It was funny when you started and I was the only one to see it. Now there's customers here. It ain't funny no more."

"I'm not here to please *you!*" she shot back, whipping her Bible around in his direction. "You're a corruptor. A peddler of filth. I know what you're doing, you hear me? You got the

Devil in you. The Devil, that's what, you been watching this filth and now you're trying to spread it around, trying to spread that ol' Devil around –"

"Now, Ethel, just calm down a minute –"

"*Filth*, you hear!" The words were sudden, sharp, like they'd been shot out of a rifle. "It's gone on long enough. Long enough!"

The hate and insults didn't faze Bobby. He kept his head down and moved around to her back side, then put one hand on each of the librarian's shoulders, and pushed her out of the horror section, back towards the front of the store. The whole way, she never shut up for a second. Just yammered about God and the Devil and the eternal battle between the two of them, and of course her pivotal role in saving the human race from being spit roast in the fires of hell.

Bobby shook his head, rolled his eyes a couple of times. By the time they got close to where we were standing, his wry countenance returned.

I watched the whole scene with little more than amused curiosity. As she went past Ethel stared at Mom, and Mom stared back, but neither one of them said anything. It seemed like the moment was almost over and I could get back to my regularly scheduled trip to through the Movie Place.

Then, on her way out the door, Ms. Stanton lifted her Bible into the air one last time. She muttered something to the sky that I couldn't quite hear, then cast a final glance at me. For ten long seconds she stood and stared, watching me. She didn't say anything but by that point she didn't *have* to say anything. I knew what she was thinking.

Then Bobby smacked the window in front of her face, and she stalked away. I figured she was pretty pissed as she left, but as I would come to find out, that wasn't the half of it.

THE CARNIVAL

"It was pretty weird," I said to Jasper that night, while we sat on my living room floor, about to get deep into my VHS of *The Terminator* for the bazillionth time. "She was going on about how the movies were gonna make everybody crazy, turn us all into mass murderers or whatever. She kept waving her Bible around the whole time. Like it was a sword, and we were dragons."

"Dragons?"

"Yep. Dragons."

"Well. Huh."

Jasper nodded. I could sense the gears moving inside his brain, but he let the conversation lay there for a moment while he pushed the videotape into the VCR.

He laid back on the floor and put his hands behind his head. "That lady's crazy. Everybody knows. I wouldn't worry about it." As he spoke, he stared at the television. For the next few minutes, he never looked at me. Just kept staring up at the television. He did that a lot when he was deep in thought, talking to me without actually looking at me. I always figured it was easier for him to do two things at once if he only made eye contact with one of them. If his eyes and mouth could work on different thoughts at the same time.

"I'm not worried about it," I said. "I just thought it was weird, that's all." I leaned back myself, resting my shoulders against the firm upholstered cushions of my parents' couch, which was covered with an ugly floral pattern that always reminded me of Audrey II, the man-eating plant monster from the musical version of *Little Shop of Horrors*.

From the television screen looming above our heads, the familiar FBI copyright warning faded into view: blurry white text shimmying against a dull bluish background that had become jittery with too many replays of the tape.

Soon after, the opening sequence of *The Terminator* unfurled exactly as we had watched it unfurl so many times before: heavy with an almost absurd amount of mid-1980s atmosphere. Smoke. Lasers. Hunter-killer mechs, hovering above the apocalyptic landscape of post-nuclear Earth. Human skulls crushed under the tread of sentient death machines. Soldiers with headbands. *Yes. Yes. Yes.*

"Yeah. She's crazy. For sure," said Jasper, not looking away from the movie. "I'm kinda sad I missed the whole show, to tell the truth. You may never get to see something like that again, being called the Devil and all."

"She didn't call me the Devil –"

"She basically called you the devil."

"Nah, she wasn't talking about anybody in particular," I said, spreading my arms out and working my neck backwards until the top of my head touched the couch. Then I snapped back straight. "Just the movies. You know how that is, sometimes people in a certain state of mind get all wound up and they barely even know where they're standing, much less who they're talking to."

Jasper wasn't impressed. He shook his head, laughed, and said, "She was talking about you. You know she was. I'm sure sorry I missed it."

He turned his attention back to *The Terminator.*

We watched for a few minutes, up through the part where slo-mo Arnold breaks down the first Sarah Conner's front door, sights her down with that laser scope, and blows her away right there on the carpet of her own living room.

"You know she's just trying to scare people," Grady said after the scene had died down and we were both itching to start our conversation back up about Ms. Stanton and her Bible-slinging ways. "She's the type that can't be satisfied unless she's making life miserable for the rest of the world."

"Yeah, I suppose," I shrugged.

After that, each of us got lost in the movie. We stayed up and watched a few more flicks – *The Lost Boys, Escape from New York, Aliens, The Thing, C.H.U.D., Halloween II* – and by the time we fell asleep it was almost five in the morning.

I can't say what time Jasper got up the following Saturday, but the clock had rolled pretty well into the afternoon by the time I managed to climb out of bed. Two-thirty, to be exact.

That messed up our plan to get to the county fair early enough to beat all the lines, so we just said "Screw it," and decided we'd head out after it got dark and experience the fair by the flashing light rainbow of the midway.

Big mistake.

We arrived at the fair just after nine o'clock, which gave us plenty of time to walk the grounds before the whole show shut down at midnight.

Mom parked the car in a grassy field near the Demolition Derby ring, then walked us through the entrance.

We first came to that staple of every small town American fair, the Arts & Crafts building. Mom told us she would be in there for the night, which left me and Jasper free to roam for the next little while so long as we promised to come back to the A&C for a check-in every hour. And promise we did, then headed for the midway.

In the late 1980s the Seward County Fair was not unlike all the other little fairs that pitched tents outside of small towns across America. I'd even be willing to bet that the scene is much the same nowadays, on certain nights in early autumn when the weather's just taking its first bite at your cheeks and the last lightning bugs of the season float careless through the air in one slow, final waltz before the cold finishes them off for good. I'd bet that for sure.

I read in a book one time that no carnival comes after Labor Day, as if that were some sort of mystic rule, steadfastly observed by carnivals throughout this mighty land. I'm here to tell you, it's just not the case. The carnival comes when it wants. On its own clock, at its own speed.

Nor is it the case, as I read in that same book, that carnivals arrive only at dawn. I swear – and Jasper can back me up – that the fairs of our youth *never once* observed either of these rules. Never once. I'm not sure what that says but it surely says something.

They always opened up in the early fall, and they always slithered into town under the cover of dark, as though they didn't want their secrets spilled by the daylight. Which is probably closer than to the truth than most people would ever like to know.

And so it was, that particular night in the middle of September of nineteen hundred and eighty-eight.

The sensations of the midway greeted us with familiar, comfortable warmth.

Sticky sweet cotton candy by the gob, hot dogs and fair burgers sizzling on the concession stand grills.

The blare of prerecorded calliope music, the *ching ching ching ching* of game bells, the joyful cries of children as they circled 'round on fiberglass unicorns and dragons.

The great cacophony of the carnival.

Down the way, flashing signs announced BULLET and OCTOPUS, SCRAMBLER and TILT-A-WHIRL.

Small light bulbs, strung around poles ten feet high, cast muddy illumination that did more harm than good.

Fluorescent pinks and blues smeared across the sky didn't help, either.

The clunky arms of heavy machinery lurched in and out of the shadows like the tentacles of those towering indescribable monsters straight out of H.P. Lovecraft: Cthulhu, Ghatanothoa, H'chtelegoth – different names for the same terrible pain crawling up your spine.

Even from up close, you couldn't exactly see the goings-on but you could see enough. You could hear the machine groans, the gnashing of metal on metal, and all that together was plenty to set your nerves on fire.

Somewhere in there, that juvenile laughter from the merry-go-round's unicorns and dragons gave way to delirious teenaged screams. Kids barely old enough to think about a driver's license found themselves hurtling helpless through space, barely strapped in to twirling metal ovals emblazoned with flames and shooting stars. Teenagers and machines shrieked in unison, the teenagers for their lives, and the machines for their lives, too. One loose bolt, one broken joint, one snapped safety chain, and everybody went to the junkyard together.

But that was all in the distance. We could see it from where we stood, but we weren't quite there yet.

Before we got to the rides, a number of games greeted us, presenting ample opportunities for winning such wonderful crap as iron-on Corvette patches intended only for the most stylish of denim jackets, candy-colored stuffed brontosaurs so large it was comical, and faded t-shirts of rock bands like KISS or Molly Hatchet who had peaked in popularity five or six years prior.

Much of the merchandise looked like it probably came from the flea market up the road in Winchester, but that didn't seem to matter to all the folks who'd lined up to take their best shots at winning little Suzy and Johnny the mottled Pink Panther of their dreams.

(Of course, me and Jasper knew the games were all rigged. For example, the metal milk cans were half-filled with cement and couldn't be knocked over without aid of a large diesel engine, much less a softball thrown by the hand of a ten-year old kid. The basketball hoops were approximately one quarter inch in diameter bigger than the basketball itself, which meant the legend Larry Bird himself didn't stand much chance of making more than one out of twenty shots from fifteen feet away. And so on.)

Carnies workers barked their come hithers – "RIIIDE THE BUULLLET!" "TAKE A WHIRL!" "MERRY GO ROUND FOR ALL THE KIDS!" – but me and Jasper tried our best to stay away from those folks. They looked, and smelled, like greased Hell, and it always seemed likely to me that way too many of the carnies who worked this fair had a history with the law that they'd prefer not be known by the general public.

Among the standouts: the two Tilt-A-Whirl operators who both possessed a mighty odor of cheap bourbon, a cotton candy vendor with a swastika on a chain tucked into his short-sleeved carnival uniform shirt, and the guy who ran the merry-go-round with a tattoo of Puff the Magic Dragon covering most of his right forearm, which would have been somewhat kid friendly (at least compared to the rest of his scuzzy compatriots) except for the fact that the dragon's smiling head had been cleanly severed and lay at his feet in a pool of cartoon blood.

Steering clear of the carnies seemed like a sound game plan. We didn't have much trouble sticking to that plan, either, just avoided eye contact and kept pressing forward.

After a quick stop at the concession stand for sugar-coated funnel cakes and approximately one half gallon of Coco-Cola each, we wandered to the back edge of the midway, to what was the actual reason we showed up to the fair in the first place.

The Kick Booty.

There aren't enough adjectives to properly describe the otherworldly awesomeness of the Kick Booty, but I'll do my best.

First, you have to understand that when it came to every other ride on that midway, all the money you could gather in your hat and your brother's hat, too, wouldn't get me to climb on a single one. They were deathtraps, plain and simple. Some parts so thick with rust that you wanted to get a tetanus shot just for walking past.

At start and stop they groaned like wounded elephants in their last pitiful throes of life, and even when they ran full speed they still clacked and clanged in such a way that hammered my every last nerve.

Every year, when the carnival rolled into town, I saw the disassembled rides pass by on flatbed trucks. The second Sunday of each September, those trucks would come in off the East Kentucky Parkway, cut through Sewardville and make their way up Highway 15 to the Seward County Kiwanis Club Park. Every year, I'd been standing there on the sidewalk in front of the Seward County Bank, watching them pass. And every time, I saw the same images in my brain: twisted metal. Fire. Broken bones.

Not the Kick Booty, though. The Kick Booty held sway over me. I pretty much thought the rest of the rides were tragic accidents waiting to happen, but not that one. It resided in a special place, above all the rest. It called to me, and every year, I answered.

Not because it was cool – it was, in all truth, the complete *opposite* of cool. Some folks might've even called it downright strange, if not mildly offensive. Others would consider it more akin to a baroque, quasi-religious nightmare.

Jasper and me fell somewhere in between those two opinions. More than anything, we just thought it was funny as hell.

In the proper sense, what we called the Kick Booty was officially known as the Atomizer, for reasons I neither know, nor care to know. It was a single row of eight fiberglass cars, each one holding no more than two adults, with an open front that allowed the riders' legs to swing freely.

The cars sat on a straight rail that was maybe thirty feet long, and when the ride started, that rail went up on pneumatic lifts and spun in a slow circle that no one between the ages of, say, three and one hundred and three years old would consider dangerous in any way.

It barely stirred up enough breeze to blow your shirt up your back. I'm, not kidding. You went up, you spun around a little, then you came back down.

I know. Sounds like the lamest ride in the world, right?

Wrong.

First of all, while you were spinning in that slow circle, the loudspeakers roared with the sounds of 1970s and 80s hard rock, which as everyone knows, was pretty much the pinnacle of human musical ability. KISS, Slade, Quiet Riot, Twisted Sister, Van Halen, Foreigner, AC/DC. (Make no mistake: there's a certain surreality listening to a Southern fried sermon to the tune of "Hells Bells.")

The rock music wasn't the only thing that the Kick Booty had going for it, either.

Like I said, the sign might have officially referred to it as the Atomizer, but everyone I knew called it the Kick Booty, after the words that marked the zenith of the psychotic sermon that ran on a loop across the loudspeaker for the ride's duration.

Against a steady electronic drumbeat, a middle-aged Southern preacher's voice recited his convictions in a slow, twangy baritone that began

at room temperature and gradually rose to full fire
and brimstone:

> *JEE-sus*
> *my friends*
> *is the way*
> *to your sal-VAY-shun!*

> *Love your NEIGH-bor*
> *Look to the car directly in front of you*
> *If you see a friend*
> *Ask if they know JEE-sus*

> *HOLD ON to your seats*
> *Hold on TO THE PERSON NEXT TO YOU*
> *REPENT NOW OF YOUR SINS OR*
> *FACE ETERNAL DAMNATION*
> *now KIIIIICK BOOOOOTY!*
> *YES!*
> *KIIIIICK BOOOOOTY!*

At each "*KIIIIICK BOOOOOTY*" the riders
were supposed to rear back and kick the seat in
front of them as hard as they could. Some did,
some didn't. I tried it once, reared back and cut
loose hard as I was physically able, and thought
for sure I'd splintered every bone between my
foot and pelvis.

So yeah. The Kick Booty was my favorite
ride at the whole fair and there wasn't even a
close second. So when I heard that ministerial
baritone boom above the fair like thunder over an
ant arm, I knew the night would be a good one.

To our surprise, the line was short. Truth be told, there was barely any line at all, just a couple of girls that looked to be around nine years old and a teenaged couple that appeared more interested in sucking each other's lips off than they were stepping up to any carnie ride, even a ride so sweet as the Kick Booty.

The last few strains of "*Kiiiiick boooooty!*" faded into the jingle jangle atmosphere of the fair, and the ride slowed to a stop.

Smiling patrons lifted the safety restraint bars from their laps, got up, and strolled back into the clamorous Seward County crowd from which they came.

Me and Jasper stepped around the kissing couple – they never had stopped sucking each other's face, not even long enough to take a breath, as far as I could tell – and made our way to the operator just as the previous ride ended and a few haggard souls stepped off and wandered back into the crowd.

We were about to climb into our seats for the Kick Booty experience when a familiar voice cracked out from the darkness.

"Grady Claremont. Jasper Bohanon. I see you out there. *I see you*, you hear? You got the Devil in you!"

That sanctimonious screech. Ethel Stanton. I could see her finger stabbing in the dark, shooting those righteous lightning bolts our way.

What I couldn't see was Ms. Stanton herself. She was nearby, for sure, but under the hazy fair lights I couldn't make out much more than shadows once my view edged out past the gravel walking path of the midway. The sound of her voice unnerved me, but not being able to lay eyes on her even as he could hear that ratchet old woman's calling my name, well, that just made the heebie-jeebies crawl up my spine all that much faster.

"You got the devil in you!" she screeched once more.

"Holy hell. That sounds like Ethel Stanton," Jasper said. I could hear the sudden discomfort in his voice, too. "What do you suppose she's doing out here —"

"Don't you boys worry about what I'm doing here!" she spit from the darkness. "The question is, what are *you* doing here?"

I squinted, looking towards the far corner of the ride's boundaries, just beyond the railing that separated the fairgrounds from the rest of the cow pasture.

For just a second, I thought I saw a little old woman in the shadows, her Bible in one hand, the index finger of her other pointed straight at me. But before I could be certain she was there, the shadows shifted and absorbed her back into the darkness.

I looked for her a moment longer, but she never reappeared. Never said anything else, either.

Still her words echoed in my head.

You got the Devil!
What are you doing here?
You got the Devil in you, boy!

*

The next Monday, me and Jasper arrived at school and learned that Ethel Marie Stanton was no longer employed by the Seward County public school system.

I wish I could tell you that the folks in charge had caught wind of her mad ravings at the Movie Place and the Seward County fair, but the truth is, she'd been foaming at the mouth for years and everybody in town knew it.

And technically speaking, I guess she still held employment with the Seward County school system for that day and a few more days after that. She just didn't show up for work, that was all. Not Monday, not Tuesday, not any day that week. Not any day ever again. Eventually, I suppose, they dropped her off the payroll and there was probably some sort of police investigation, although I didn't pay much attention to the news to see what was going on with that.

All I know is, I saw Ms. Stanton on Saturday night at the fair. I was waiting in line at the Kick Booty, she was slinking around in the dark, wagging her self-righteous finger and spouting off at me and Jasper. Then I didn't see her again.

Not for a couple of months, at least.

SOULS

Now let's take a minute, and go back a ways.

When I was seven years old – we're going back a few years now, well before my run in with Ethel Marie Stanton – Uncle Teddy let me watch my first horror movie. His house featured the first satellite dish in all of Whistle Mill, and you better believe I took full advantage of that, spending a lot of my younger days over there soaking up movies that I otherwise couldn't have seen, no way no how. (This was in the last days of the Dark Ages, otherwise known as the years right before the big VHS boom of the mid-1980s.) I feel confident saying that Mom would have kicked Teddy's ass up one side of Main Street and down the other if she'd known about it, but then again she probably would have kicked his ass about a lot if she ever heard tell of what he was showing me in those days. Which, she never did hear tell, and as far as I'm concerned, that's probably best for everyone involved anyway.

For a scary movie loving kid like me, visiting Uncle Ted's place was like visiting a fantasy land of candy canes and cinnamon gum balls. There was so much sweetness to be had, laid out right there in front of me; all I had to do was make sure I didn't eat too much and go home in such bad shape that Mom never let me go back.

Even though I was barely past kindergarten, Uncle Ted let me stay up 'til one or two in the morning, longer if I could keep my eyes open. It's hard explaining just how much this contributed to my upbringing. As it turns out, I was an all-time champ at keeping my eyes open whenever it meant I could watch movies the likes of which Mom would never allow in our house. Mostly a lot of horror and science fiction flicks: *Dragonslayer, Hell Night, Pieces, Conan the Barbarian, Invasion of the Body Snatchers* (the Mr. Spock one), *Poltergeist, The Funhouse,* plus the occasional R-rated action movie of which I mainly remember a couple of Sylvester Stallone classics, *First Blood* which everybody's seen and then another called *Nighthawks* where Sly grew out a full beard and in one scene, a dude is running and gets his face sliced with a blade. That's about all I remember of that one other than Billy Dee Williams was in it, too. I suppose that I just never cared for action movies unless they had some sort of sci-fi or monster element, like *Predator* or *Aliens*.

But regardless of what Mom might have had to say about it, Teddy's house was the place where I watched my first horror movie, and that's a fact.

It was a Saturday night in October, and my uncle had gone to bed. I was laying on the couch by myself, watching The Movie Channel with all the lights in the house turned off. A movie came on that was clearly labeled RATED R and even though I never had the prior occasion to know what RATED R meant, I got the distinct impression from the downshift in the announcer's voice that little boys were supposed to change the channel right then and there before the horrible, nasty, vulgar movie came on and fried their little impressionable minds but good.

Still, no matter what the announcer said, I didn't change the channel. That RATED R movie began, in kicked the screaming and the special effects, and before long I was positively enraptured by every last second of it all. Never looked away, not even once. Now, don't get me wrong, the whole spectacle scared the absolute hell out of me. Frightened my Boba Fett underoos plumb off, I ain't afraid to admit.

And as I also ain't afraid to admit, I liked that feeling.

Hair poking up from the back of my neck.

My heart thumping in my ears.

My mind racing out of control.

In the quiet parts of the movie, I could hear the house breathing. Sighing and sagging in the midnight, the way old houses always do.

I wondered if there was something behind me, in the shadow-shrouded corners, waiting. Maybe just outside the window, waiting. Waiting for the right moment, the perfect time to burst in and get me and carry me off to a terrible, bloody ending.

The screen flickered, the house whispered its ominous threats, and I thought about these things.

I had never felt this way before, but I liked it.

And what movie did this to me?

The Howling.

It also was the first time I ever laid eyes on a naked woman, so I guess there's that, too.

The Howling revolved around a TV reporter lady who checks into a weirdo psychiatric camp outside of Los Angeles after she gets attacked while chasing a story. Of course it turns out she's not at a psychiatry camp at all, but what I can only describe as some sort of weird New Age werewolf colony. The story goes a little haywire from there – the reporter's husband gets bitten and turns into a werewolf, the whole colony comes after her, and as she's escaping she ends up getting bit, too.

Looking back on it through my grown-up eyes, the story had this wacko, fuzzy vibe to it, lots of psychiatric horse hockey and such, but mostly played with a sly wink like, *hey, don't take any of this too seriously, kids.* Besides that, *The Howling* had everything to scare the crap out of a little kid: hairy monsters with big teeth and claws, a decent amount of gore, and a badass man-to-wolf transformation scene that for sure badassness, I'm here to tell you, it beat anything in this world that I'd ever helt, smelt, or felt, at least up until that point in my seven-year-old life.

What I'm saying is, I learned a lot thanks to Uncle Ted.

Horror movies aren't the only thing he introduced me to, though. He also taught me the value of knowing my history, and also of knowing my ghost stories.

"Do you know where this town got the name Whistle Mill?" he said to me one night, as we sat around after turning the TV off. Uncle Ted lounged in his favorite old beat-up recliner. That thing was ugly as all get out if you asked me, covered in rough plaid cloth that contained all the colors of autumn, shades of brown and orange and a stray green here or there.

I occupied the matching couch, propped up in the corner nearest my uncle, chin resting comfortably in hand. We sat cattycornered to each other, just a couple of feet apart.

Around us, there wasn't any sound except the creak in the walls, and the crickets chirping outside the window, but it was still enough to fill the silence that temporarily spread into our conversation.

"No," I said. "Do you where it came from?"

Teddy's face dropped. "Of course I do, son," he said.

He glanced out the window, into the night.

"Part of it," my uncle continued, "is 'cause of the old lumber mill that used to sit right outside of town. At one time, that was the biggest business in the whole county. Hell, it employed half the people around, until they eventually closed it on account of dumb asses kept getting their arms and legs sawed off up there. You'd think they'd know, it's a lumber mill, you gotta be careful about where you put what parts of your body. But some people just don't wanna pay attention, I guess.

"Anyway, that's the 'Mill' part. I bet you actually did know that, didn't you?"

I nodded, and Uncle Ted returned the same gesture.

"Most people do," he said. "But the 'whistle' part, well, that's a different story. I bet your mama never told you that one."

I shook my head that no, she hadn't.

"Of course she didn't."

I sat up on the couch. "Why wouldn't she?" I asked.

Uncle Ted's voice dropped to a whisper. "Because this is the dark country, Grady. Your mother never cared much for living out here."

He nodded.

I leaned forward.

"Mmm-hmm," he hummed. "The dark country."

That was the first time I ever heard that phrase – *dark country* – but it wouldn't be the last. It sounded perfect, capturing everything that I felt about the landscape around us in just two simple words. *Dark country*. The shadowy acreage, the bare tree limbs.

For the rest of my life, I kept that phrase close.

"Well, I'm gonna tell you what your mama won't. They call this place Whistle Mill because on some nights, when the weather's just clear enough and their ain't no wind rustling the leaves around, you can hear the souls of the dead, making their way across the grounds, and the sound they make as they go is like a whistle. A low, long whistle. Not loud, now. Not loud at all. Matter of fact it's so quiet that you can't hear it unless you listen careful and a lot of times, not even then.

"Some people say the whistle's the sound of dead men breathing, pushing out whatever air's left in their lungs before those lungs rot away, like the noise a balloon makes when you stretch the opening out too wide. Other people say it's more like a train whistle, shrilling on a cold, foggy night, announcing there's a ghost train at the station ready to pick up whatever spirits are ready to travel off the mortal plain. Yeah, I've heard both of those stories. More than once, too. In all honesty, though, I don't much believe either one."

Now, Ted had me. I was locked in to his every word and he knew it. He let me sit there for a second, stewing in my own childish anticipation.

"Have you... have you heard it?" I whispered.

He nodded. "Sure I've heard it," he said. "More than once, too. And can tell you this for sure, it ain't no train. It ain't nobody breathing.

"I've heard the whistle that gave this ol' burg its name, and I can tell you what it is *exactly*: it's the sound of souls. That's what it is. Souls, making their way out. Souls floating off to Heaven, or Hell, or just out there with the stars. Out there with the dust. Out there with infinity.

"But any way they go, they're gone, Grady. Gone, you hear? When the whistle blows, all them souls are outta here. And when they're gone, they leave behind nothing but the used-up bodies that once was our friends, our neighbors and our relatives, but now ain't no more than husks. Empty as a rag doll with all the cotton insides pulled out.

"When the midnight comes and the air situates just right – just like it is tonight, actually – that's the sound you'll hear: that old dead whistle, sounding its dead tune, its tune for the lost, for those that are leaving this world, and those that have done left it a long time ago. If you hear it, you know death's nearby. And if it ends up getting somebody besides you, don't get to feeling too much of a relief. Sooner or later, you'll hear that whistle again. One of these times it'll come back and it won't leave 'til it takes you for a ride. That's just how it is, nephew. Best get ready."

Only four years later, in that sticky summer of nineteen hundred and eighty-six, Teddy was gone. Yanked from the Earth by the banshee of Boone Creek while me and Jasper stood there, unable to do anything about it.

When you're a kid you think grown-ups will go on forever and stay just the same as they are in your youth. I learned differently, that one night in July. I didn't hear the whistle then but I saw death come just the same.

I wasn't ready then, and didn't know if I ever *would* be ready.

Not long after that, we faced the horrors of middle school..

The back half of the nineteen eighties began quietly enough for us. Sixth grade flew by, but nothing happened of any great import. We made the transfer to the new school and went about our way just the same as we'd gone about our way in our years at Whistle Mill Elementary. Horror movies, *Fangoria*, Marvel comics.

I've reflected on that sixth grade year often during these last few decades. And every time I've thought about that period of my life, I've become more convinced that those few months, the fall of '86 through the summer of '87, were the last real year of my childhood – the last year we were really kids. The last year we did whatever we wanted, whenever we wanted. Our last year of abandon, playing with G.I. Joes and watching movies and reading science fiction and horror books. Doing whatever we felt like for no other reason than that's just what we felt like doing. We weren't worried about the rest of the world, or how exactly we might fit into it.

It was the year before our voices cracked. Not just literally – the hormones saw to that for sure – but also in that most poetic of ways, too, if I can be so bold as to use that word. Our inner voices cracked that year, too. Not just in timbre but in thought. Not just in tone, but in feeling. Not just how we sounded but how we *wanted* to sound. How we wanted everyone else to hear us.

I think Jasper felt the crack first. Soon after Uncle Teddy's death, he said to me, "Infinity ain't a point on a line. It's *every* point on *every* line. It's not just possibility, it's *all* possibilities." He could sense something inside that brain of his. He knew change was coming, I believed that then, and I still believe it.

He was right, too. Of course he was right. Voices crack. Things change. You change.

DARK COUNTRY

Much like sixth grade before it, the first couple months of seventh grade went by on a largely uneventful scale, outside of the sudden disappearance of Ethel Marie Stanton. (We got over that easy enough, anyway. Never overestimate the value of a self-righteous old librarian in the lives of middle schoolers.)

After the Seward County Fair, autumn rolled on past. School happened but there wasn't anything eventful about it. I spent the weekdays of September and October staring out classroom windows, watching dead leaves twirl in the air, while my teachers droned on in the background about subjects I didn't care about like Algebra and U.S. states and capitals. Occasionally a lesson would catch my attention – like Halloween week in Literature class, which we spent reading *Something Wicked This Way Comes,* that Ray Bradbury story about Cooger & Dark's traveling Pandemonium Shadow Show – but more often than not, I'd just watch those leaves tumbling away to nothingness. That, or I'd lay open the latest issue of *Fangoria* into my textbook and read about horror movies instead.

Me and Jasper spent every weekend of that fall just like we spent most every other weekend since we'd met: picking out movies at the Movie

Place, popping up popcorn, and sharing stories we'd either read or heard about. Every now and again, we'd relive the night in '86 that Uncle Ted had been visited for the first and last time by his banshee. Most times, I'd throw careful glances towards the window just to be sure the specter hadn't made her terrible return. But as far as we could tell, the banshee seemed content to stay away.

The school days didn't get any more interesting but the weather sure got a heck of a lot colder. Thanksgiving Day brought a record cold for the date, with a high temperature every bit of 3 degrees above zero. Then we hit December and eventually fall gave way to winter.

As I recall, December of that year brought the sharpest, coldest weather we'd had for any early winter in my lifetime. For the first half of the month, the temperature topped freezing once. *Once.* Six inches of snow fell on December the twentieth and it pretty much stayed there until well past New Year's Day with a fresh top layer of the white stuff piled on every couple of days. Schools across Seward county were closed all but seven days between Christmas and Valentine's Day; mostly they were closed on account of bad roads, but a couple of days were lost to busted water pipes at Whistle Mill Elementary, and one other day, a prankster broke into the high school and wiped shit – human shit *and* dog shit – on every chalkboard in the building.

A couple of weeks before the snow hit, on the one day when the high temperature managed to break the freezing mark – and by "break the freezing mark," I mean it was a whopping thirty-three degrees out – me and Jasper went for a stroll back through the trees around the deep end of Martin Holler Road. That might seem odd to some, a couple of seventh graders walking alone through the bare woods during wintertime, but you gotta remember, this was out in the country in the 1980s. People didn't worry about child murders and abductions and crazy drugged-out whackheads back then the way they do now. Me and Jasper spent a lot of our time in the woods, playing when we were kids, philosophizing when we got older. Our parents just told us, "Be careful," and made sure we didn't forget our heavy coats.

That Saturday didn't start out any different than any other Saturday – Jasper's dad dropped him off at my house just before noon, and we sat around talking about the latest *Iron Man* and *Fantastic Four* comic books. And of course, he had already gotten his hands on the new issue of *Fangoria*. Seems like he always got his before I did.

As we thumbed through the pages, I noticed my friend didn't quite seem like himself. He'd laugh at a joke and even make one or two of his own, but still he just seemed to be missing something. Long stretches went by with both of us staring silently at still photos from *Halloween 4*, and normally that would have been a perfect opportunity for discussion.

I tried. "Looks like they're finally bringing back Michael Myers."

Jasper nodded.

"You know, *Halloween III* wasn't so bad," I said. "It might not have been what people were expecting, androids and killer Halloween masks and all that, but I still thought it was pretty cool."

Jasper shrugged.

Whatever was going on, I couldn't pin it down.

We went like that for a few more minutes, until I decided that maybe we should find a change of scenery. If Jasper had something on his mind, I wanted to find out what it was. Maybe he would tell me if we could get a little further away.

Now, by this point, me and Jasper hiked a lot. It was just something we started doing, probably because the woods around us were quiet and nobody ever bothered us out there, and then kept doing it because it suited us just fine. Our parents weren't too keen on the idea of us tromping about on our own, and at first one or another Mom or Dad insisted on joining our excursions. We'd find cover under a rock ledge or a tree canopy and set up for the night, and wouldn't worry about the elements as long as we could keep the fire burning. Most times we'd stay up until dawn telling stories or kicking around one philosophy or another, so that fire never was in any danger.

Eventually, the two of us got as familiar with the woods on that end of the county as we were with our own backyards, and the adults in charge relaxed a little. As long as they knew where we were headed, they generally left us to ourselves.

So, that Saturday, I asked Jasper if he wanted to go hiking. He just shrugged – he was in a shrugging mood – and I took that as an affirmative. Then I asked Mom if she could take us out to Martin Holler, hoping that would get us far enough away that Jasper might open up a little.

Martin Holler was ten miles further east than Whistle Mill, out past Duncan's Mill, into what Uncle Ted called the "dark country." Plenty of that shadowy acreage and bare tree limbs. It was in the end of Seward County where most of the civilization melted away into a sea of trees and scraggly fields, cut through by the occasional gravel road. Every so often, there'd be a house or a barn, maybe two or three together, but nothing much more than that. Whistle Mill wasn't urban by even the loosest of definitions, but compared with the backwoods of the dark country, our little town looked like a megalopolis.

It took a fair amount of convincing on my part. Mom didn't seem in too permissive a mood that day, for reasons I didn't know and never did find out.

It was too cold, she said.

She had too much to do around the house to drive us out there, she said.

It was too far for us to walk ourselves, she said.

I had an answer for everything. We had heavy coats. Thick boots, perfect for outdoor travel. We'd dress in layers, wear toboggans. We wouldn't be outside *that* long. She could drive us up the holler and pick us up when were through.

After a solid hour's worth of this back and forth, Mom finally relented. She agreed to drop us off on her way to the grocery store. We agreed to be back in the same spot beside the road two hours after that, so she could pick us up on her way home.

A little while later, me and Jasper had on our heavy coats and an extra pair of socks in our boots, and we were making our way through the woods. The temperature might have been thirty-three, but the air still had bite. A cold dread seeped up from the ground, too, clinging against our shoes, biting our ankles and toes, pestering us. All those prior days of cold had kept the ground frozen solid and one day above freezing wasn't near enough to thaw everything out. Each step we took in the wooded depths of Martin Holler made a crunchy sound like peeling a dead cat off a frosty lawn.

As we walked, I could tell something was gnawing Jasper around the edges. He stared at the ground, not sayin' anything, which wasn't his normal way at all. Earlier in the day, he'd been plumb chipper, but now, I couldn't dig a word out of him with a bulldozer and a shovel.

I left him alone for a few minutes, but eventually that dead-cat-peeling sound of our footsteps got to be more than I could stand.

"You gonna be okay?" I asked.

"Yeah," he said.

"You sure? You're awful quiet."

"Yeah," he said. Again. "I'll be fine."

He wasn't fine, though.

"You went awful quiet on me," I said. "Now I'm wondering if we came all the way out here just to listen to ourselves breathe."

Jasper didn't answer. He stopped, took a deep breath, and exhaled what seemed like all the hope of his soul, which was what he always did when he found the subject at hand especially peculiar. I knew something must be percolating in that brain of his.

The wind picked up for a moment, flipping a few brown strands of Jasper's mop hair down into his eyes, which he brushed away with one hand.

We stood there a few moments longer. My friend stared into the trees, and finally said, "I saw her last night, you know."

"You did? Really?" I didn't want to admit it, but I had no idea what he was talking about.

"Yeah." He paused, as though he knew that I still didn't understand. "Ethel Stanton. I saw her last night."

"The librarian? Where?"

"Up there." Jasper stared at the sky, held his gaze there as he took a few more steps, then looked back at me. His slow stride never broke the whole time.

We walked.

"Well, not exactly up there," he continued. "More like 'out there.' I saw her standing cross the road from my house. Just looking at me. So weird."

"Did you talk to her?"

"I couldn't."

"Why not?"

"She disappeared."

"Where'd she go?"

"Out there. Like I said." He waved his right arm out in front of himself, then above his head, around in a circle. *Out there.*

He glanced in my direction, but turned away just as quick and kept walking. I was pretty sure he sensed that I was falling further behind in the conversation with every word he spoke.

A few more seconds passed, with no sound in the woods of Martin Holler except the rustle of dead leaves in the breeze and the steady crunch of the ground beneath our boots.

Are you sure you really *saw her?* I thought. *It seems so weird, that she's been gone all this time and then would just turn up walking out by your house –*

"I know, it seems weird, right?" Jasper asked. "That she's been gone all of this time and then just turns up out by my house? Just walking down the road, like nothing ever happened?"

He said that.

He said exactly what I had been thinking. Word for word.

"It's been bothering me ever since. I only saw her a few seconds, then she was gone. But I know it was her. I'm as sure as can be of that. You know what I think she was doing?"

He paused to let me answer, but I didn't.

"I think she's wandering," Jasper continued. "Wandering through this world, the world she knows best. As far as we know, we were the last two people to see her. Maybe she's still tied to us. Just like that banshee was tied to your Uncle Ted."

The thought didn't strike me as all that comforting. But, it made sense. If Ethel Marie Stanton had moved on to the great Out There that Jasper was talking about, and we were the last people she saw on Earth, maybe a part of her still wanted to reach back to our plane, back towards the last hands she saw before she left it. Our hands.

Maybe.

"Or maybe not," Jasper said.

Dammit.

"Maybe she's wandering around out there, and she's come across some of what else is out there, and she's got lost in it all. She's not here but she's not there. She's stuck in between. She don't know where to go. I've considered that, too."

He stopped walking.

"I've been reading, Boo. There's such a lot of… things… out there. I don't what else to call them, but *things*. I don't think there's even words to describe what all lives outside our world. They're not what you'd call nameless, because there's no name that could ever be given to them. Un-nameable, that's what they are. And Out There, that's where they are. We can't see them, but they can see us. The Boone Creek Banshee, old Ethel Stanton, part of the same. Moving between their world and ours, never quite in one or the other, always in between both.

He paused. Thought about it.

"Always in between. Never fully in one place or the other. Sounds a lot like you and me, don't you think?"

ME AND JASPER AND THE
LADY IN THE WOODS

We got the rest of the way through middle school, then ninth grade after that – our first year of high school. The world kept right on turning. Me and Jasper haunted the Movie Place as much as ever. *Total Recall, Gremlins 2, Bride of Re-Animator, The People Under the Stairs.*

Neither one of us ever attended another Seward County Fair, but later on, Jasper did swear he'd seen Ethel Stanton a couple more times, strolling silently down the road in front of his house. He never managed to take a picture or otherwise find a way to prove she'd actually been there, but hell, how much proof did I need? This was Jasper Bohanon.

Then, in late 1991, everything changed.

Jasper got his driver's license.

When you're sixteen, life don't get much better than that moment when you walk out of the clerk's office holding that magical piece of plastic in between your sweaty little fingers. Your driver's license is a ticket and when you got that ticket in your hand, you got freedom. Freedom like you ain't never known before, freedom like you never even knew existed. I'm talking about

Freedom with a capital "F." It flows through your veins.

You think it's gonna be great, sure. But you got no idea. Never having to ask your Mom and Dad for a ride. Always being able to go where you want, when you want. Growing up without having to actually be a grown-up. That's freedom. What else could you call it?

Jasper got his learner's permit in early November, just a few days after his sixteenth birthday. His license came a month later. Got it on the first try, in fact, which I thought was pretty damn impressive – managed a perfect score, too. Up until that point I'd have told you that a perfect score wasn't possible. Hell, I'd been for my test twice already and still hadn't cracked sixty percent. Second score was worse than the first, and the instructor even went so far as to suggest that I get used to the idea of public transportation. I suggested he choke on a fat one, which didn't portend too well for my third try, but you know how that is.

Jasper's dad had promised his son a car if Jasper brought home a totally clean score on the driver's test, and I'm sure he was surprised as anybody when that actually come to pass. Still, Mr. Bohanon was a man of his word. Jasper got what he was owed.

Thing is, there evidently wasn't a lot of preparation that went into the fulfillment of that promise, and not a whole lot of cash, either. Later on Jasper told me that he thought the car cost his dad fifty dollars and a box of twelve-gauge shotgun shell, and in all honesty I didn't see any evidence to deny that.

My friend's car was a seventeen year old Gremlin.

If you know anything about cars, you know that the AMC Gremlin was one of the all-time turdbuckets that ever rolled off an automotive assembly line, an auto industry abomination whose name could pucker any true car lover's rectum when mentioned to this day. Being seen in a Gremlin was like having a haircut three years out of style. When you went by, people mostly just gave a polite nod, waved and kept their laughter to themselves in the interest of common decency. Mostly.

They haven't made those cars for decades and far as I'm concerned, they never should have started in the first place. Saying it was a piece of shit might be the understatement of the millennium; actually that would be an insult to all the pieces of shit that have passed across this mortal coil down through the ages.

It was two-tone orange, with a white stripe running through the center of the hood, over the roof, and down the trunk, split up only by the front and back windshields, both of which had more cracks than surely was legal. All the hub caps were gone, and I guessed they had been since the Carter administration. The passenger's side door was busted shut. The car probably hadn't seen a decent wash since Reagan, either.

Worst of all – and this was the feature of the car that would always define it, as far as I was concerned – the floorboard was riddled with rust to the point that when it was rolling, you could see the yellow road lines shoot by underneath. Some of the holes were clustered in small groups where not one was bigger than a BB. Other places, there was gaps big enough that you could put your fist through. I never felt sure that it was completely street legal to drive a car in that kind of condition, but still, Jasper drove it and I rode around with him so I guess it doesn't matter that much in the grand scheme of the universe. Anyway if you ever ran over a copperhead or a rattlesnake you'd just lift your feet in case the snake got any ideas about coming in through the gaps. It beat walking.

Jasper even gave that old car a nickname: Gizmo, after the furry little mogwai from the movie. I told him he should call it Stripe – partly on account of the white racing stripe across the hood and partly on account of the fact that in the same movie, Stripe was the name of the main evil gremlin –– but I didn't get a vote in the matter.

Despite the fact that Gizmo wouldn't win any car shows or impress any ladies, that car was Jasper's and nobody else's and that meant a hell of a lot to a sixteen year old boy in those days. Probably still does.

The night after he passed his driver's test, Jasper pulled Gizmo into our driveway. When he honked the horn. It made a sound like the fart of a dying mule.

"Who is that?" Mom said, pulling the sheer blue curtain back so she could peer out the kitchen window.

I walked over next to her, looked outside, even though I didn't really need to. "That's Jasper," I said. "He got his license today. We're gonna ride around."

"You're gonna what?"

"Ride around."

"Ride around where?"

"I don't know. Around."

"Around." She waited. "Huh."

We stood there, still just looking out the window.

"In that?"

"Yeah, Mom. In that."

"Well, I hope it's got some good brakes," Mom said. "That's important." She walked away.

Meanwhile, Jasper hit the horn again. Already, the mule didn't have much life left. All Mom could do was shake her head.

"You sure it's safe?" she asked again.

I didn't know one way or the other, but I knew what she wanted to hear. "Sure, it's safe," I said. Then, I bolted out the door before she had a chance to ask me anything else.

We drove down Main Street, listening to the sickly whir of Gizmo's engine, a sound that made me wonder if maybe a mouse had somehow gotten into the engine block and died and his dried out mouse parts broke up and blew through the valves just enough to make that irritating little noise, but not enough to shut the engine down. I even asked Jasper if he thought there was something wrong, as diplomatic as I could without outright saying that his car was a piece of junk and might already be on its deathbed.

He didn't much give of an answer, so I let it drop.

We pulled into the parking lot of the Big Wheel convenience store, in a spot only ten feet away from the entrance. Right next to a brown '85 Firenza with a half-assed purple window tint job. We'd see that same later that night, up Martin Holler.

"We gotta get to Martin Hollow tonight," he said, soon as his wheezy old gremlin rolled to a stop.

One thing about Jasper Bohanon, he always took care that he said certain words proper; a particular one was "hol*low*," where the rest of us in that part of the country said it "hol*ler*." Not every word, though – just the ones that everybody else seemed to mispronounce on a regular basis. He'd make it a point to show he knew we had it wrong and he had it right. His theory was, if you sound like an idiot, you're bound to get treated like an idiot. I wouldn't argue that point, either – I just didn't give a rip either way.

"Martin Holler?" I said.

"It's 'hollow.'"

"I always heard it pronounced 'holler.'"

"Holler. Uh-huh. Well, that's perfect for the locals but it ain't much for the King's English."

I wanted to remind my friend Jasper that he was every bit as local as me, and maybe he ought not be so holier-than-thou with his words, but I didn't. Wouldn't do no good anyway. Instead, I blew on past.

"Why are we going up there?" I asked.

"Does it matter?"

"Hell yeah, it matters." I didn't want to just take his word for it. "It's gonna be ass chilling cold tonight," I said. "I ain't going out in the ass chilling cold with you or anybody else if there ain't a good reason. If you can't tell me why we're headed up there, I'd just as soon stay where it's warm."

Jasper shook his head and let out a little breath to signal his disappointment. Then he said, "Gonna make camp, that's why."

"Make camp? Did you not hear me? It's supposed to be near twenty degrees tonight."

"Yeah, I know that."

"Our nutsacks will freeze against our legs –"

"Nah, they won't."

"They will!"

"They won't. Our sacks will be just fine. You're actin' like an old lady."

He turned off the engine, sat there for a second, and then opened the door. When he did, a bitter wind come roaring into the vehicle, cutting me like new scissors through old paper. I could have done without it.

"I'm going in here to get some coffee and lighter fluid," he said. "We'll build us a fire, it'll do the trick. Trust me, Boo. We gotta go tonight."

I didn't like the sound of that. "We gotta?"

"Because," Jasper said. "From what I can tell, the Lady is gonna be out tonight."

"The Lady?"

"You know. The Lady of the Woods."

Okay, that got me excited. The Lady of the Woods had been on our radar for a while. Far as we were concerned, she was up there with the Boone Creek Banshee, and I'd heard Uncle Teddy and some of the older folks tell tales about her on many a night when the bonfire roared and the beer overflowed from dozens of red plastic cups.

I'd heard about a lot on nights like that, though. I never knew what was supposed to be real and what wasn't, and after a while I quit trying to figure it out. But if I'd learned anything from our experience with the Boone Creek Banshee, it was that some of Uncle Teddy's tales were more than just stories.

Maybe more than some.

"Bull," I said.

"Nope, not bull at all. Real as real can be." He pushed the car door open the rest of the way, letting in even more cold air, and held it there with one hand as he said, "I got it on good authority that there's gonna be a real live witch showing up in Martin Hollow tonight. We're going."

Before I could ask him just whose authority he was speaking of, Jasper climbed out and slammed the car door behind him. He had to slam it three times before it actually latched shut. I couldn't help but laugh a little at that.

He never said nothing else, though. A few seconds later he was gone into the store.

That left me in the car by myself. I watched Jasper walk through the Big Wheel, down the first aisle. Directly in front of where we parked, he struck up a conversation with a girl I recognized as Evie Fallon.

She was a wispy little brunette, barely five feet tall and thin as frost on a morning lawn. She wore a white long-sleeved Kentucky Wildcats sweatshirt, and over that an acid-washed denim jacket that was the same shade of indigo as her blue jeans, which were peg rolled at the bottom. Her molasses–colored hair hung clean and straight, and went about halfway down her back. She kept her bangs teased into a loose ball, something like a radar dish perched in front of her forehead. (That had to be about the most popular hairstyle among all the girls at school in those days. I wondered on more than one occasion if they were transmitting messages back and forth with those radar dishes, sharing sordid secrets about Aqua Net hair spray, and Jordache jeans, and Bon Jovi concert t-shirts.)

I wouldn't say that Evie was what you'd call gorgeous – at least I wouldn't call her that, anyway – but she was pretty enough, I guess. She had a sharp little nose, and a bright, easy facial expression that never seemed to convey anything but bouncy happiness. Pretty, like I said, but nothing to make a man lose sleep over.

Except for her eyes. I'll admit, her eyes were gorgeous. Weird, almost. Big and light gray, and glittering almost silver when the light caught them just a certain way. I never saw eyes like that before and I haven't seen any since, either.

Other than the way she looked, though, I didn't know much about Evie. That's the honest truth. Jasper was friendlier with her; they lived on the same stretch of Cotton Creek Road, and had ridden the same school bus from kindergarten into high school. He told me once that their Moms and Dads played poker and drank whiskey shots together every other weekend and sometimes more often than that. Now that Jasper had his driver's license, I figured she'd get a ride to school in Gizmo from time to time. If she could stand to be seen in it, of course.

Right then, Jasper pointed out the window, towards me. I could tell from the gestures he made with his hands and eyes that he was talking her into coming with us.

Under normal circumstances, I would have been a little put off that he invited her to go with us – I didn't care too much to spend my Friday night with somebody I barely knew – but at that moment I was already resigned to heading up Martin Holler and lost in wondering just what we'd find there. Evie barely registered in my mind, otherwise I would have told her it'd be best if she just went on home and left the witch hunting to the big boys.

I would come to regret that later. Maybe not in the way you might think, but I'd regret it, sure as the world. A lot might have been different about that frigid night if little miss Evie Fallon

would have just tromped her little ass out of that
Big Wheel and caught a ride back home with one
of her other friends.

But she didn't.

Instead, she came outside with Jasper,
smiling and a be-bopping around like she had
corn for sale, and sashayed around to my side of
Gizmo the Gremlin, where she motioned for me
to roll down the window. Which I did, just a
crack.

"Hi," she said, leaning her face in towards
the opening.

"Hi, Evie."

"Y'all going up Martin Holler, I hear."

I nodded, glancing at Jasper. "Yeah, we were
talking about it."

"You boys're going up there tonight lookin'
for a witch, aincha?"

"We aren't looking for anything," I said.

"Sure you are," Evie giggled. "The Lady in
the Woods. You don't really think I ain't heard
about her?"

Of course she'd heard about her. The way
this conversation was going, I half expected her to
tell me they played rook together on Tuesdays.

"Where'd you hear about that?" I asked her
anyway.

"Oh, you know how it is," she laughed. "You
live around here, you hear things from time to
time."

I nodded, and shot Jasper another look,
trying to let him know that I didn't much care for
the idea of Evie Fallon joining us that night.

Before I could get that point across, though, she stood back up and shoved her hands into the pockets of her denim jacket.

"Well, if you are or if you ain't gonna look for her, I'm still gonna meet you boys up there," she grinned. "Don't worry, Jasper said it's okay. I hope it is by you, too."

I didn't give her an answer, but then again I knew she wasn't asking for one. Anyway, I didn't have time anyway because she hightailed it off to her car – that sorry-ass '85 Firenza – and took off before anybody could get another word in.

Before we go any further, I need to tell you about Evie. I said I didn't know much about her, but I didn't say I knew nothing

One thing I can tell you about Evie Fallon is that she grew up on Cotton Creek Road, barely. I say barely because she lived far enough back in the country that there was hardly any road at all. Her parents' place was the last house before the road turned to gravel and the county quit offering maintenance. Any time they got a pothole, it stayed there until it either got big enough to swallow the school bus, or Evie's dad hauled a wheelbarrow full of concrete mix out there and patched that thing up himself. He ran the Ace Hardware in town. Evie's mom taught at the middle school. The three of them lived in a little mint green A-frame at the end of Cotton Creek Road and as far as I could tell, they were all good people.

Other than that, like I said, I didn't know much else about the girl. She was more Jasper's friend, and as far as I knew she was probably the only friend he had other than me. But besides knowing that she lived out at the far reaches of Cotton Creek, I also knew one other fact about her. I suppose it was the only thing that counted.

Evie loved *Fangoria* magazine.

Let me say that again.

Evie Fallon was a girl, and she loved *Fangoria* magazine.

To say that a girl loved *Fangoria* in those days was like saying a boy fancied bubble baths with Barbie dolls. There probably were a few other odd ducks out there like that, but... well, you know. If they were out there, they surely weren't interested in making themselves known to the rest of the world.

All except Evie. She didn't give a damn. She loved *Fangoria*, blood and guts and all topics horror-related. Had every issue, read them cover to cover, could refer at will to specific paragraphs in specific articles. She could describe every cover in depth, from the main photo to the smaller headlines on the film strip down the side.

Number nine. *Motel Hell.*

Number ten. *Scanners.*

Twenty-three. John Carpenter's *The Thing.*

Sixty-one. *Rawhead Rex.*

Seventy. *Pumpkinhead.*

Sometimes we'd make a game out of calling out issue numbers and seeing who could name the cover story first. It was always Evie. I knew a

lot about *Fangoria* but not like she did, because
she was a human Dewey decimal system when it
came to referencing that magazine. I'll just be
honest, it still seems hard to believe even as I'm
telling you right now. But believe it you should –
because it's the honest truth.

I never saw much of her until high school.
But then, in ninth grade, she started joining me
and Jasper during noon break. We'd gather in the
high school's main lobby, off in one corner, and
crack jokes about the football players and how
they were always wearing t-shirts two sizes too
small, trying to make their muscles pop out, but
instead just highlighting the fat rolls in their
bellies.

Between jokes we'd talk about whatever
seemed interesting at that moment, the new *Friday
the 13th* or *Nightmare on Elm Street.* Maybe the new
David Cronenberg movie. Occasionally, Stephen
King would have a new book out, and we'd kick
that one back and forth, talking about where it fit
on his list of top books, which was usually
somewhere above *Christine* and below *'Salem's Lot,*
but nowhere near *The Stand* which was at the time
and still is to this day the best damn book ever
put to paper by human hands.

No matter the topic, Evie always seemed to
be out front of it. I'd read an article about *Pet
Sematary* or *Silence of the Lambs* or *Nightbreed,* and
ask Jasper whether it was worth seeing, and
before he could get a word in, Evie would tell us
that she'd just been to Lexington the weekend
before with her Mom and Dad, watched it,

thought it was okay. (Her Mom and Dad seemed to be big horror fans, too.) If it was a book, she'd already read it, thought it was okay. Just okay.

That was pretty much her review on everything – "okay." Never great, never awful, just a shrug of the shoulders and "okay." Then she'd launch into a detailed monologue about whatever she'd seen or read, which would take up the rest of that day's break time. On the one hand that aggravated the piss out of me, but on the other hand, it was pretty damn impressive.

Still, those few minutes every day at noon break were the only time I ever saw Evie Fallon. I guess Jasper saw her a little more often than that.

We ended up in Martin Holler just as we'd planned, but something happened on the way that took all the words out of Jasper's mouth. He never said a thing for three whole hours, and when I tell you what caused it, I think you'll understand.

I said before that Martin Holler Road was a gravel route, but that's not quite a hundred percent factual. To tell the truth, the road up that holler was no more than a leaf-covered dirt road with two tire tracks wore in it, from years past when the big logging trucks rumbled through the mud and hauled off what little timber was worth taking. Like I also told you before, there really wasn't no shoulder at all, but a worn strip of dirt at the edge of a weed field that ran parallel.

Gravel or no, shoulder or no, it was a

heckuva rough ride. We bounced along until Jasper spied Evie's turdish Olds Firenza.

"There she is," he said, pointing towards her car with his index finger. He pulled Gizmo onto the road's sort-of shoulder, and cut the engine. Then he switched off his car's headlights and we got out. As soon as we did, my face took a windy blast. For a second I considered the idea that maybe this little excursion wasn't such a hot idea, but when I saw Jasper stepped out of the car that same wind smacked him upside the head and he never flinched, I decided to suck it up. If he could take it, I could take it.

We grabbed our tents and our backpacks, which were loaded down with full supplies of marshmallows, potato chips, and water. Then we set about to find a proper place to camp.

Bear in mind, Jasper hadn't said a word for a while now.

"Don't you worry, we'll find her," I said again. "We'll find Evie."

"Maybe," Jasper whispered. "Maybe we will, and maybe we won't." He kept walking.

So what happened to Evie Fallon, between the time we saw her at the Big Wheel and the moment when me and Jasper arrived at Martin Holler to find her empty car?

It's kind of hard to explain, but I'll do my best. After she left us at the Big Wheel, me and Jasper went back to his house to pick up a few items that we forgot early in the afternoon A couple of flashlights and his Dad's .22 pistol. That still gave us enough time to swing by the I.G.A. to pick up some other various and sundries.

Just as we were pulling out of Jasper's driveway, who else but Evie come tear assing in there. She parked her Firenza right behind us so that we couldn't go anywhere even if we wanted, then hopped out of the vehicle with the car's engine still puttering.

Her silvery eyes were wide open now. Her breath came in heaves. I didn't know what spooked her, but from the looks of things I felt sure she'd seen *something*. She was moving our way so fast, and those radar-dish bangs of hers was bouncing around to such a degree, that I feared not even the mighty power of Aqua Net superhold hairspray could save them from collapsing asunder.

Somehow the dish held, though. "Jasper! Grady!" she gasped, running at us as we descended the steps from the front porch, headed towards Gizmo. "You ain't gonna believe this, you ain't gonna believe, I saw her, I saw her already –"

"Who?" I asked.

"I was on my way here, and she skittered across the road, up into the woods –"

Jasper put one hand on each of Evie's shoulders, trying to settle her down, but that girl was spooked so bad there was no settling her at all. Still, he tried. "Calm down," he said, "Take a deep breath. Tell us again what you saw."

Evie inhaled, closed her eyes, and waited a

few seconds before she said anything else. It wasn't much, but it settled her down enough that she could talk and make sense at the same time.

"I saw the Lady," she said.

"You what?" me and Jasper said together.

"I saw her. I did."

"That's interesting," said Jasper. "She's supposed to stay around Martin Holler. Never heard of her coming over this way."

"Well, she did."

"Can you take us to her?" I asked.

"Sure," she said. "You want me to ride with you?"

I took one look at Jasper's beat up Gremlin and pictured the three of us riding down the road, cramped together, with my knees pushed up against the dashboard. The car was small enough already, but with our gear in the backseat it would get even smaller.

"Nah, you drive, and we'll follow," I said. Evie agreed with that plan and a minute later we were on the road.

As we pulled away, I looked out the back window and saw Uncle Teddy's old dog Henry walk up onto the porch and lay down in front of Jasper's front door, with his head resting on his front legs, just staring at us as we left. Right before we turned onto the highway, I saw that hound lift up one front leg and bury his face underneath, like he couldn't bear to watch whatever came next. I hoped that wasn't one of those harbingers that Jasper always talked about.

*

We tailed Evie a couple miles down the road, and I was thankful that there wasn't any other traffic out. I didn't know for sure what we were getting into and I'd just as soon that we not get into it with any other folks who might not have the same open minds that we did about any potential otherworldly experiences.

About five hundred yards from the turn to Martin Holler Road, Evie pulled her car onto a wide gravel shoulder. There wasn't enough room for two cars, but Jasper managed to squeeze Gizmo off the asphalt far enough that I felt like we probably wouldn't get run over if another vehicle come by. Probably.

Evie jumped out and pointed into the woods that waited just a few feet beyond our cars. "There," she said. "She come across the road and then went into the trees right there."

Jasper slammed his car into park and threw the door open, exiting the vehicle in such a hurry that he forgot to shut the engine off.

"You sure it was her?" he asked, as he gazed straight into the woods, down the same direction that Evie pointed.

"I don't know who else it could have been," she said. "She ran across the highway, right in front of me. And I swear, right before she got to the grass, she turned and looked right me."

Up until then, I sat in Jasper's Gremlin, watching the two of them talk about the situation. The Lady wasn't there at that moment; I didn't see the need to spend a bunch of energy that I'd probably need later if we actually *did* come across her. But when Evie said she'd made eye contact with that old hag, that statement got my interest.

I got out of the car. "What'd she look like?"

"Like nothing else you ever saw," she said.

I didn't know if Jasper had ever told her about our run-in with the Boone Creek Banshee, and I didn't want to bring it up if he hadn't. So I didn't say anything.

"She had a face like a wasp's nest," Evie went on. "Gray and cracked, peeling at the edges. Her eyes was black, and sunk way back in her head, like they was set back in a deep well. She had dirt rubbed all over her skin, and in her hair, too, which was ratty and full of twigs and leaves. I wasn't close enough to actually smell her but if I had been I'm pretty sure it would have been like walking around in a cow pasture during the summertime."

Jasper laughed. I didn't think it was that funny but I gave it a half a grin, anyway, just to be a good sport about it.

"You know else?" Evie asked, looking at Jasper.

He just looked back at her, so she tried me next. "You know what else, Grady?"

"What's that?"

"I saw her teeth, too. She flashed 'em at me, the same way a raccoon flashes its teeth whenever you get one backed up to a fence. I swear to God, she had a hundred teeth if she had three. They were all filed to a point, too, like a mouthful of shark's teeth, only a little bit smaller and nowhere near as clean."

I was formulating my response – and wondering just how clean a shark's tooth might actually *be* – when something rousted around in the woods, fifty yards or so in the same general area to which Evie and Jasper were already directing their attention.

"You don't think –" I started.

Before I could finish, she was there.

The Lady herself.

And she looked familiar – at least I got a sense of something familiar in the gray blur that whipped around us. But nothing sure.

What happened next flashed by so quick that it was all over before any of us knew it even started. None of the three of us had enough time or presence of mind for any real reaction, either. I'm telling you that right now because when you hear what came next, your first thought will probably be, *Why didn't they just get the hell out of there?* My simple answer is: we flat-out weren't able. Believe you me, if we could have, we would have. But we couldn't, so we didn't.

So here's how it went down.

The old woman didn't appear from those woods so much as she exploded out of them, the way guts explode out of a deer carcass that's laid out on the side of the road for too long. As that wicked lady tore through, dead tree limbs and leaves swooshed outward in every direction, helpless to stop her rush forward. Remembering it now, the whole scene puts me in mind of old A-bomb test footage like we'd watched in history class, black dirt swirling around, spindly trees bent over until their tops touched the ground.

This wasn't no A-bomb, though. This was the Lady of the Woods. Every bit of her. She flew out of the trees on a rail, screeching the whole way to beat the Devil himself. The awful sight and sound of her oncoming rush put me in mind of one serious bullet train from Hell, a supersonic missile of sharp fetid teeth and untamable strands of filthy hair riding the winter winds straight out of whatever blackness might spawn such a beast.

She headed right for us, in fast-forward, screaming cackling howling horror. And we watched her, and we knew we'd had the lick this time for sure, and there wasn't one of us – not me, not Jasper, not Evie – that made one move to stop it from happening. That witch was gonna get us good.

And then she stopped.

And when she stopped, I finally got a good look.

It was Ethel Marie Stanton. More or less.

Sure as all get out, it was her.

She screeched right to a dead full halt smack in the middle of the road, like she was flying on a string and all her string just completely ran out, all laws of physics be damned. The dirt still swirled behind, the trees still bent to the earth, slowly bowing back up, but there she was, standing on the asphalt, separating me from my friends across the way. A wispy smoke trailed behind her, already vanishing into the dusky air.

I smelled something like burnt plastic.

She turned her head around sharp, towards Evie's Firenza.

Lifted her hand and waved towards the sky.

The Oldsmobile went flying, up into the air, over the trees, out of sight. I never heard it come back down, either.

"Holy hellllllll –" I whispered under my breath. But before I could say or do anything else, the wicked woman raised her hand again, this time towards my friends. Again she waved her fingers, not much motion at all, just a flick at the sky.

Jasper crumpled to the ground, instantly unconscious.

Evie lifted into the air, spinning in a tight circle, just like somebody was pulling her up on a steel cable. She started screaming. "HELP! GOOD GOD, HELP ME!" and yelped on into frantic gibberish as she kept getting higher. And higher. And higher.

The Lady spun back to me, flicked her other hand in my direction. When she did that, I felt my legs buckle beneath me. The world started darkening around the edges. Then it wasn't just the edges, but the whole damn thing, sinking from the light. As I fell and everything slipped away, I heard the screams of Evie Fallon, soaring over the trees, headed for God-knows-where, and I had no idea whether I'd ever see her or anyone else again.

*

The next time I opened my eyes, it was pitch black outside. Jasper was bent down beside me, pushing on my shoulder in an effort to roust me up.

"Come on, Boo," he said. "Come on now, we gotta go find her –"

I scrambled to my feet. "Where'd they go?"

"I don't know yet."

"Evie? That... thing?"

"I told you, Boo. I don't know."

As we ran back to the air, I gasped for words. "Did you see her face? Did you see who –"

"Sure, I saw," said Jasper. "I saw plenty." He got to the car, ripped open the door and jumped inside, never mentioning Ethel Marie Stanton's name. Not that it was necessary by that point.

Then we were in the Gremlin, bouncing along the rough road up Martin Holler. I watched just outside the light of the headlight beams, looking for something to dart out of the darkness.

Remember how I told you we came across Evie's '85 Olds, the one that was the color of a dusty turd with a bad purple tint job in the rear windshield? Well, it's true, unlikely as that might seem given the run-in we'd just had with the Lady of the Woods, who I now knew was none other than Ethel Marie Stanton.

But find Evie's car we did, sitting right there on the road shoulder in a spot where there wasn't much shoulder at all, just a worn patch of ground at the edge of a weed field. Just sitting right there, pretty as you please, despite the fact that the previous time we'd laid eyes on that car, it was flying across the sky like it was held with together with toothpicks, chewing gum, and aluminum foil.

So yeah, I was surprised to see it in such a spot. I was even more surprised to see that it didn't have a scratch or a dent one on it, as if it had been gently placed there by the most caring, careful of hands.

Jasper parked Gizmo next to that strangely safe, well-parked car. We jumped out, grabbed our belongings from the backseat, and walked into the tree line, determined to find Evie and face down the Lady of the Woods, who we now knew was real as real could be. Damn right she was.

Forward we went. Jasper barely said a word. We were both wired enough as it was, but the silence between us ratcheted the night up even more. I said a few encouraging words of the "She's gonna be all right, we'll find her" variety, but I could tell Jasper wasn't listening. I couldn't blame him; besides, by then I already knew that when Jasper got dialed into something, he didn't hear much but his own mind, whirring.

Eventually, we spotted a blazing bonfire, set back deep in the holler woods and burning bright, weird green flames unlike anything else I'd ever laid eyes on in this world. On one side of that fire was the Lady, dancing around and braying up a wicked storm. And on the other side of the fire, just barely visible through the flickering flames, I could see Evie, lashed by her waist, wrists, and ankles to a big oak tree with what appeared to be barbed wire and thick, dead vines.

That's when matters somehow got even more interesting.

ME AND JASPER SAVE EVIE
FROM THE DEAD

We worked our way through the trees, doing our best to not make any noise that might draw Ethel Stanton's attention before we were ready for it to be drawn.

In the shadows around the fire, I saw she had something else tied up beside Evie: a monster twelve-point buck deer. The animal was held fast the same way as Evie, with barbed wire and thick brown vines, braying something awful. He gnashed at his bonds with everything he had, too, but it was plain to see that he wasn't going anywhere. Part of me wanted to yell out, "Hang on, big fella! We're coming!" but the rest of me knew that probably wouldn't be wise.

The Lady rendered it a moot point when she walked around the fire, put one hand around the base of each of the buck's antlers, and gave a mighty yank, separating head clean from body.

Yes, she did that. Didn't look like it took any real effort on her part, either. She got herself a good handle with those wicked, bony fingers of hers, and ripped that deer head free from its sinewy moorings just as easily as a little kid might pull the head off a grasshopper.

The poor deer kicked a couple more times before he finally squealed his final breath. By

then, there was a lot of blood on the scene. A *lot.*
When the Lady of the Woods wrenched the
buck's head from his shoulders, that hot red goo
sprayed out of the stump like water from a busted
fire hydrant. Even though the sky was black out
that night, with no moon to light our way, in the
bonfire's emerald glow I could still make out the
geyser of red grue as it showered the Lady and
even splashed over on Evie, too.

The Lady of the Woods didn't seem to mind.
She let out a satisfied cackle, smearing deer blood
all across her face.

Evie wasn't quite so pleased when the blood
come her way; she screamed, horrified, and I
knew she had to be wondering if she was resigned
to the same fate as the dead animal that lay
nearby.

Jasper froze. I did, too. I'm not ashamed to
say, I didn't know what to do first, puke or run.
Looking back on it I admit that neither was really
a good idea since drawing the Lady's attention at
that point wouldn't have served any purpose
other than getting us all killed. We were gonna
make a move, sure. But we had to do it when the
time was right.

So the hag picked up that severed deer head -
chunky meat and part of its spinal column
dangling free from the base of the ragged neck
stump – and held it up like she'd just won the
Super Bowl and this was the trophy they gave her.
Then, she reached up into the viscera, rooted
around until she found something she liked (I
couldn't tell what exactly, since it all looked like a

blurry, bloody mess to me), and spread it all across her clothes. She had her reasons, I guess.

After that, she opened up the poor animal's mouth. Yanked its tongue out through the bottom of his neck, and held it up for a second, too, the meat dangled limp over both sides of her hand, glistening in the weird fire light. Then, just in case the whole scene wasn't awful enough already, the Lady cut loose with a wretched laugh that was jagged enough around the edges you probably could have used it to cut down a pine tree. She bit into one end of the ripped-out tongue, and held the gory thing there fast while she stretched it out with her hand as if was nothing more than a piece of sweet cherry taffy. Stretched it all the way out, she did. All the way out, that is, until it snapped clean in half. The smaller piece that was left between her teeth, she swallowed that whole. The rest got tossed into the green flames, which roared with hellish pleasure at the witch's flesh offering.

About the time that tongue disappeared into the fire, Evie passed clean out. I can't say as I blamed her.

To say that I'd never seen the like, well, that's a bit of an understatement. And I'd hate to speak for my friend Jasper, but I feel pretty safe in saying that he'd never seen the like either. Who had? But there we were, up in the bowels of Martin Holler, face to face with our old librarian Ethel Stanton, the Lady of the Woods, and we were the only thing that stood between that witch and the soul of our dear friend, Evie Fallon.

Well, Jasper's friend. My acquaintance.

We had to make a move, but at that moment, neither one of us was sure what that move might actually be.

While we were pondering on that, the Lady saw us. She let out a vicious scream, not unlike the scream of a jet engine taking off from an aircraft carrier, and hurled that deer head our way. It came to rest on the ground not two feet from where we stood, tumbled to a stop in a perfect upright position and stared up at us with its dead black eyes. The mouth hung open, too, and some gooey blood dribbled out, and I thought about the fact that the tongue should have been there, too, except for the fact that it had been ripped out and cast off already.

Anyway, it didn't look good.

And then the Lady came towards us.

As soon as the witch made a move our way, me and Jasper took off in different directions. I cut around the right side, thinking I could circle around and get Evie. While I did that, Jasper rushed straight at the witch. I wasn't sure what he thought such a move might accomplish, but there wasn't a lot of time to ponder on it.

Whatever his reasoning, the move distracted her. Jasper drew her full attention towards him, and that gave me the cover I needed.

I crashed through the woods, swatting tree limbs from my face as I went, but still kept my eyes on that green fire and Evie behind it. After what felt like an hour but probably wasn't more than ten or so seconds, I reached her.

As I set to freeing Evie, unwrapping the barbed wire from about her waist and wrists that lashed her to that big oak, I realized that it wasn't barbed wire at all, but thick vines, curled tight and hard. Truth be told, barbed wire would have been easier to unwork.

Before I started pulling the vines away from Evie's wrists, I checked Jasper and made sure the situation was still under control. As under control as it could be, anyway.

He'd run to within a few steps of the fire and stopped. Now, he stood there, glaring at the witch even as she had him sighted down, too. They looked like two cats with their backs arched and their tails straight up in the air, ready to claw each other's eyes out.

I turned back to Evie. "How'd you manage to get tied up like this?" I asked, breathing heavy from the run but also from the effort of working through those vines.

"If I knew that it probably wouldn't have happened in the first place," she answered quickly, in a soft voice that I could barely hear. She did her best not to draw the hag's attention, but even at that, I could tell Evie's nerves were just about shot.

As she talked, her voice sped up and she had to fight to keep it quiet. "I just woke up here. I pulled off the road with you and Jasper, and the next thing I know I was spinning in the air, watching you guys get smaller and smaller below me, and then I blacked out. Then, I wake up here. Can you go any faster?"

"That's Ethel Stanton, you know," I said.

"I didn't notice."

"Well, it is. If you get a good look at her face, you'll see –"

"It was a joke. Of course I noticed. How could I not notice? Can't you cut me loose any faster?"

"I'm trying –"

"Try harder!"

I did my best, and after a few more seconds it seemed like her bonds were getting looser and the thick, tough strands easier to untangle.

I glanced at Jasper, saw him and the Lady closing in on each other, and knew it would be just a few more seconds before everything went full-on ape shit. *More* ape shit, anyhow.

Finally the vines came loose. No sooner had they been tossed into the fire than Evie leaped away from the tree, wringing her wrists, with a look on her face like she didn't know whether she was coming or going or what she was gonna do whenever she got there. We looked at each other for a second, wondering what we should say. But, what *can* you say in a moment like that?

As it turned out, we didn't need to say anything.

"Get over here, Boo!" yelled Jasper, a few yards away, in the thick of the trees. Me and Evie looked over there at the same time, and saw the Lady was just a couple feet away from him. But, weird thing was, she'd stopped. Dead stopped.

While Jasper stood there staring at her, the hoary Lady of the Woods lifted her hands to the sky, threw back her head, and started murmuring syllables that didn't much sound like any language I'd ever heard.

"Oksana-bay-ul... oksana-bay-ul... cthulhu r'yleh cthulhu sothoth."

At first I could barely hear the words, and couldn't understand them at all. Then they started getting louder, and I still couldn't make any sense out of what she was sayin'.

"Ok-sana-Bay-Ul! Cthulhu rei!, PH'NGLUI, CTHULHU! APOCALYPTO MGLW! R'YLEH NWNG CTHULHU BAY-UL! BIRDOGGA YOG SOTHOTH!"

She threw her hands out to the sides of her body. When she whipped her head around to face me and Evie, I thought for sure she'd spring at us and we were done for.

She didn't do that, though. She just fixed that hateful eye on us, and chanted away. And I still couldn't make any sense of it.

"OK-SANA-BAY-UL! CTHULHU NE BAY-UL! MAR-TI-NA NAV-RA-TI-LOVA WGAH, BAY-UL R'YLEH!"

On her unholy command, the wind kicked up. There'd barely been any air stirring up until then, but as soon as that witch uttered her spell a gale blew in that bent the spindlier tries around us almost until their top branches touched the dirt.

And then the dirt itself started moving.

A low rumble grated the night, and the ground vibrated beneath our feet. At first, it was just a small shift, a few pebbles, some dried pine needles, slipping around like you might see during a tiny earthquake. I wondered if maybe the Earth might rip apart at the seams, and swallow us all down into its fiery maw.

As the Lady of the Woods chanted –

"OK-SANA-BAY-UL! BAY-UL R'YLEH!"

–the gale winds just up and vanished, not in a low winding down but all at once, like they were coming from a machine and somebody yanked the plug. For a few seconds everything went still – the air, the ground, me and Jasper and Evie and even the Lady of the Woods.

At that moment, a worrisome fear crept into the bottom of my stomach. Something was about to happen. I didn't quite know what, exactly – but something.

The Lady laughed.

"Back away from her!" I yelled at Jasper, but he was already of a like mind, stepping backward, trying to ease himself around towards us without drawing Ethel's attention. He didn't look as nervous as I was, but he didn't look like he wanted to be too close when whatever was coming actually got there, either.

The witch raised her hands to the sky one more time, bellowed her strange syllables, shook her head from side to side as hard to she could to give the words every bit of force that she could muster.

"OK-SANA-BAY-UL! BAY-UL R'YLEH, OK-SANA BAY-UL! CTHULHU SOTHOTH! YOG SOTHOTH! PH'NGLUI! PH'NGLUI! PH'NGLUI!"

With that, the hag collapsed.

A sharp thunder crack split the night down the middle. One more time, the dirt moved. But this time, instead of the pebbles and the pine needles and the little specks shifting around, the earth beneath us heaved inward and back out, not everywhere but in a few spots, more than one of which was a lot closer than I'd have preferred.

"Grady," Evie said, her voice getting louder as she tried to overcome the ruckus sound that built around us. "Grady, what's going on –"

Before I could formulate any decent theory, both of us noticed at the same time that a hand was clawing out of the dirt just in front of where the witch lay.

A *hand.*

Jasper saw it, too. "Back off! Hold on! I'll be right there!" He tossed aside any thought of carefulness, and raced towards us, leaping over the witch and the clawing hand, too, just as that hand pushed on out of the earth and became a full arm... and then a shoulder... and a neck... and head...

Now, I don't know who that head belonged too, but I do know that whoever it was had clearly been dead for some time. Not much skin remained, just rotted scraps clung to dirt-crusted old bones. The jaw hung slack, barely connected at one hinge, frozen forever in a silent scream that would have been almost comical under less immediate circumstances. As the dead thing pulled itself out of the ground, I could see ripped clothing shreds dangling on the corpse – jacket, pants, with a small flat hat rested haphazard atop the skull – and in the green fire light I could make out that they were grey in color, kind of like a Confederate soldier's uniform from the Civil War.

Or, exactly like that.

I was still considering the notion when the ground opened up in one place, then another, and another. And from each one, another corpse clawed its way out into the open air.

As the corpses came forth, I swear I heard a low, long whistle. Not loud, not loud at all – only a steady, mournful whistle. Long and low. Long and low. The same whistling Uncle Ted told me about all those years past. The sound of death. The sound of souls.

Out there with the dust.
Out there with infinity.

I watched the Confederate soldier rise, not doubting what I saw but finding it hard to believe all the same. My doubt gave way to cold horror soon enough, as I realized what was happening.

The Lady had turned out the dead. And they were coming for us.

In the dim light, I saw a couple more dead soldiers, still dressed in the remnants of their tattered rebel grays. Even in the moment it struck me something odd because Kentucky was a Union state in the war and there actually wasn't much fighting around these parts. Not that it mattered. Here they were, and here they came.

Not all were Johnny Rebs, though. Some weren't soldiers at all and from what I could tell, some didn't look like they'd been dead nearly as long, either.

One was a woman, her decayed visage peering out from behind a tattered veil that fluttered in the night wind; she'd been buried in her wedding dress that was now just as rotted and full of holes as the girl who wore it.

Another looked like a preacher; his white collar gave it away, his black preacher's garb long faded to dull gray but surprisingly intact, more intact anyway than his poor body, which had lost both legs and one arm somewhere along the way and dragged itself along the ground by the only hand it had left – a hand with only three fingers, at that.

We didn't have time to consider where all the bodies could be coming from. This wasn't a graveyard, least not as far as I knew, anyway. Still the fact remained: the dead bodies *were* coming. Men, women, children in various states of dress and decomposition, though from the lack of headstones I assumed none had been buried less than fifty years and if you asked me to pin it down I'd guess it was probably a century or more.

The crowd shambled towards us, slack-jawed and filthy. Dried out scraps of skin and hair dangled from some of the skeletal frames. Others were nothing more than bones in funeral dress. All stared at us with black, bottomless sockets, their eyeballs long since lost to the ages and their lips shrunk away like slugs in saltwater, exposing what crooked teeth they had left in a sort of permanent dumbass grin.

I made out a few more individuals – a couple other Civil War soldiers, a farmer dressed in ragged denim overalls, a little boy and girl who surely weren't more than five years old when they died and must have been brother and sister, too, judging from the way they were still holding hands as they staggered forward in their finest Easter outfits. He in his tiny blue suit, she in her white dress with lace around the bottom, both of the outfits remarkably well kept except for a few threads at their edges. Better kept than their faces, for sure. Those were clean on one side but torn up something awful on the other, as though these siblings had been buried cheek to cheek in a final sweet embrace before the elements and insects had taken over and meshed them together over the decades, until tonight, when the call of the dead had urged them from the grave and they'd ripped themselves separate while climbing out.

For the most part, though, it was just a mess. A faceless tangle of putrid corpses. Dead folks. Undead folks – eyeless nightmares, caked with mud, run through with worms, ambling along on splintered leg bones while the air filled with the sharp stench of dirt and decay. I didn't know from where they came, fully unaware of any cemetery proper in the vicinity, and even to my uneducated eye a lot of the corpses looked way too fresh given the century-plus they'd been in the soil. (I would have thought they'd be no more than skeletons.) But it didn't matter. There they were, all the same.

I figured they had us.

The thought of a final charge came to mind. The undead moved slow, and seemed to all be in front of us. Maybe we could bust into the rotting crowd, fists swinging in every direction, and fight our way through, knocking heads off in every direction as we cut a path to freedom. Their skulls and spines had to be soft as the dirt they came from. Probably couldn't withstand a decent punch, even if those punches came from three sixteen year old kids. We might have a shot.

Then again, I'd seen the original *Dawn of the Dead* more than a few times. If the zombies got us down, they'd keep us down, overrun us, and be munching our guts in a matter of seconds. It wouldn't be pretty.

About the time I was ready to let go of that idea, Jasper appeared at one side of me. He grabbed Evie under one arm, "Let's go!" he said. She clasped her hands the back of his neck, grateful and ready to be carried away to safety.

But we weren't going anywhere.

Now the corpses came alive in waves, like fire ants bursting from their underground tunnels. Three more crawled out of the ground, then ten, then twenty. More than that. I lost count. Worst of all, there were too many for us to get past; as they shambled back into the realm of the living (or at least the realm of the living dead), they created a wall of vile decay that blocked any hint of escape. And more were on the way, too – I could see the ground breaking free in the woods behind us, rancid fingertips poking their way through the cold dirt, then hands, then arms then skulls and shoulders as more dead folks pulled themselves out of the ground.

The situation looked grim, to say the least. Just me, Jasper, and Evie, facing more of the undead than I could count. Every time I thought I'd seen the last one, another showed itself.

I looked at Jasper. "What do you think?"

"I dunno," he said. He stood there, thinking about our predicament. I could tell from the look on his face that not only did Jasper not know our next move, he wasn't sure we even *had* a next move. I didn't feel too good about our spot.

"Jasper," I said. "What are you thinking'?"

"Hold on."

"Hold on?" Evie asked him in disbelief. "What do you mean, hold on? Don't you see –"

He held up one finger, and silenced her in mid-sentence. "Yeah. Hold on."

This time, she got the message.

Evie stared Jasper down, and for a second, I thought she was gonna jack his jaw. Before she could do anything – and while I still sort of wondered how that would work out, anyway – Jasper took off on a dead run for the Lady. He never said a word, never gave any warning. Just went for her.

The next few seconds were agonizing, as I watched my friend barrel headlong towards that nasty creature. She was happy to let him come, too. His footsteps pounded the earth, thumping in my ears like cannon fire, as he ran fast as he could, head up, arms extended like he was gonna wrap in a big bear hug.

The Lady of the Woods never moved. Well, she moved some. Her lips did anyway, pulled back at the corners in a hateful, decrepit sneer that reminded me more than a little bit of that awful grin that made Freddy Krueger famous in those *Nightmare on Elm Street* movies.

I knew from that look that not only wasn't the Lady threatened in the least by Jasper rushing at her, but she surely *wanted* him to come her way.

"Jasper!" I yelled, thinking – hoping – I could catch his attention before he got himself into a spot that maybe he couldn't get out of, but it was too late.

I'd barely even opened my mouth when he dove at her headlong.

Even now, I can't tell you what Jasper Bohanon figured he might accomplish with that move. It wasn't exactly well thought out, if it was thought out at all. But whatever great idea might have spurred him into action went south in a hurry.

Jasper come flying at the hag, full on, but she didn't make any effort to get out of the way. Didn't so much as move one nasty fingernails Instead, she just kept that rotten smile plastered on her face, and extended her right hand out in front with the palm facing out to Jasper like a big STOP sign – which is exactly what it was.

Jasper's face hit that palm with about as much success as it would have gotten from a smack into a solid concrete wall. Then he crashed to the ground, and laid there. I thought he was dead for sure. I thought *we* were dead for sure.

A second passed. Two, three, four. I know because I counted each one and they were the longest four seconds that I'd experienced in my life up to that point.

Evie put her hand over her mouth and stifled an anguished scream. I thought she could fall apart any minute.

It occurred to me that with her in that state and Jasper crashed on the ground, if we had any shot of getting out of there, it was up to me to make a move, but I didn't have much time.

While Jasper was making a go at the witch, the dead bodies still shimmied through the woods, coming towards us. Some upright on two legs, others on a leg and a stump, still others dragging themselves along with just their hands or arms or whatever scraps of limbs they had left.

I saw a skinny corpse in a black dress hook its teeth in the dirt and get enough leverage to wriggle forward a couple inches at a time. The damned thing didn't have a choice, either – all its arms and legs were long gone.

I turned to Evie and said, "Stay here."

There wasn't much danger of her going anywhere at that point, but I thought it still a good idea if I told her to stay put. If she got a wild hair and thought about taking off, maybe she'd remember my words and think twice.

Once I was sure that she'd stay still, I turned my attention back to Jasper. Ethel Marie Stanton loomed over him, still with that ghoulish expression. Now I could see that Jasper actually wasn't dead, but moved just a little, pushing away on his elbows so he could get in some sort of position to defend himself.

He wasn't moving much, but at least he was moving.

There wasn't any more time for thinking about it. I followed Jasper's lead and took a run at the witch, hoping like hell that her attention would be focused enough on Jasper that it would give me all the time I needed to get there. What I was gonna *do* when I got there, I hadn't quite figured that out yet, but I reckoned something would come to me.

Sure enough, something did. As I got within a couple of steps of them, the Lady still hadn't taken her eyes off Jasper. She bent down, one hand stretched out, ready to take him by the throat. I thought that she might not have enough time keep her hand on him and stand up straight to catch me, and as it turned out, I was right.

I launched myself at her, up and through the air, a javelin. By the time she turned to face me, it was too late. My fist caught her square in the left temple, knocked her off balance and sent her tumbling backwards with an evil hiss that sounded to my ears like a pole cat facing off a copperhead snake. But she didn't go down.

As soon as he realized what had happened, Jasper got his energy back. He jumped up and threw a forearm into the witch's chest. That staggered her just enough to give us another opening. I gave her a shove, then me and Jasper hit her at once. He went high and I went low and between the two of us we managed enough force to finally take the Lady of the Woods off her feet.

And then some.

She soared up and back, a good ten feet, easy. Maybe it was adrenaline or maybe we had more strength than we thought, but either way, that old girl went flying through the autumn air and when she came down, it was smack dab in the middle of her own emerald fire.

As she landed, Jasper sprang back to his feet with new life. Less than a minute ago he skated on the edge of bad intentions, with the witch's hand closing around his throat. Not anymore. "Hell yeah!" he whooped. "We got her! We got her Grady, you hear?"

"We got her," I said.

I heard the hustle of heavy footsteps on dead leaves, and when I looked over my shoulder I saw it was Evie.

The three of us stood there together, and watched the Lady of the Woods catch one last hot ride.

When the witch hit the fire, she went right up. Man alive, did she ever. The flames climbed her ratty dress for just a couple of seconds before they ignited all at once into a wicked blaze that wouldn't have gotten any hotter any faster if she'd been filled full with dead leaves and cotton balls then soaked in kerosene. As the fire enveloped her, she let out a shrill scream, long, high, and held it while her skin bubbled and peeled back, while her ratty hair burnt up like tinder, while her eyes puffed and exploded from their sockets. She clawed at her face, ripping the fried skin loose in chunks.

Her scream went silent.

I figured she must be dead, but she wasn't, not even close. Instead, she started laughing. Laughing! I never heard the such. I'd heard a banshee wail, heard a grown man scream as his soul got ripped from his body, and both those were impossible to forget, but I swear I'd never heard anything that chilled my blood the way that hag's laugh did as she lay there in that fire in her final moments, watching her own body turn to ash.

Ethel Stanton let out a cackle like a chainsaw starting up, violent as all hell, then it faded, just as she faded.

The green flames climbed into her mouth and back out her eyes and ears and she burnt that way for a little longer before her head popped like a bad zit.

Freshly fed, the fire lit up the woods as bright as they'd been all night. We could see in that weird green glow, the same vile shade of green that we'd observed when we first showed up on the scene that night and found the Lady munching down on her wrenched-off deer head. There were dead folks still out on the ground, hundreds of them. They'd crawled out of their graves, still dressed in their funeral clothes, and dragged themselves through the woods headed for God knows what sort of foul business.

Only now, I could see – they weren't going anywhere.

Jasper saw it, too.

"What happened?" he whispered.

"Nothing," I said. "Nothing happened."

"Something definitely happened."

"Well it's not happening now," I said. "They aren't moving, are they?"

We stood there, to make sure. No, the dead weren't moving. Not anymore.

I reached out for Evie's hand just to make sure she was still there. I could see her, sure, but seeing's not always enough. Sometimes you have to touch what you can see just to make sure it's there and your mind ain't fooling.

Both of which I was relieved to find out was the case when I felt her warm fingertips dancing into my open palm.

Jasper walked out towards the corpses. They all lay on the ground now in various odd angles, collapsed where they stood without regard for us or our right of way. We had to step on top of several just to make our way back towards the car. Our walk started out careful enough, unsure as we were that the bodies might rise back up at any moment even with the witch long gone. But soon enough it became clear that they were dead once more, and so we picked up our pace, eager to get out of those woods. Brittle skulls and jaws and ribcages crunched under our every step.

Before long, Jasper broke out ahead of us, jumping over the bodies and the underbrush, headed back towards where we'd parked Gizmo.

Me and Evie did our best to keep up but before long realized there wasn't much chance of that. We pulled up, already breathing hard. Thick clouds of frosty air puffed out in front of our faces with every breath we took, and it occurred to me that in all the excitement, I hadn't realized how far the thermometer had dipped.

I noticed Evie shivering, with her arms pulled in tight against her chest and asked, "You need somethin' to keep warm?"

"Nah, I'm okay," she said.

"You sure? You look like you could use –"

"Thanks, though." She looked away from me. "I'll be fine."

Of course I knew that wasn't true. I took my jacket off and gave it to her anyway, and from the way she yanked it out of my hand I knew she was grateful.

We walked on.

I figured we'd catch up with Jasper whenever we caught up with him. There didn't seem to be any urgency to the rest of the night. The Lady of the Woods no longer posed any threat, as she still smoldered in the emerald fire behind us. I briefly wondered if we ought to go back and put out the fire for the sake of safety and Smokey the Bear, but we let it go. It was already burning itself out, anyhow.

We talked on the way, not much more than whispers. Seemed like both of us were still in shock, the electricity in our brains dialed down and not quite ready to spark again just yet. I asked Evie questions I thought she wanted to hear and she did the same for me and neither one of us put a lot of thought into the process.

Do you think they'll come back?

Probably not.

Where do you suppose that old witch came from?

There's no telling.

What's gonna happen when somebody comes across all these dead bodies?

I couldn't say.

Somewhere down deep, legitimate questions longed for the asking. We'd get to them later.

A few steps from the ridge, something caught my ankle. I took a heck of a spill and while it didn't seem too serious – "Watch yourself!" Evie said as I went down – the landing was hard enough on my shoulder that I didn't think I could spring back up for a little bit. I squeezed my eyes shut, rolled over on my back, and laid there and waited for the pain to ease

As it subsided, I reached out and absently ran my hand along the cool ground. When my fingers brushed against something stiff, bigger than any rock or tree limb, my eyes shot back open. I just knew that I'd hit a dead body.

Which I had.

Uncle Teddy.

I didn't know how he got there.

I wasn't sure I even *wanted* to know.

After the Boone Creek Banshee got the better him, we'd said our goodbyes and buried Ted in the family cemetery. That was a good five miles away. He couldn't have crawled that far in just the time the witch built her fire and raised the dead from the ground; we'd been there for all of it and it couldn't have been more than twenty or thirty minutes, nowhere near long enough for a freshly reanimated corpse to dig itself out of the soil and amble from there to here. He probably couldn't have done it that fast when he was upright and breathing.

I jumped up, wanting to yell something, anything, but all the sound had been shocked out of me.

"What is it?" Evie asked.

"Uncle Ted."

"*Your* Uncle Ted?"

"Yeah." I took a breath. "Mine. Damn. Who else's?"

She came over, next to me. "Your uncle, the one the banshee got, I suppose. I thought you told me you guys laid him to rest in the graveyard behind –"

"Cemetery."

"Huh?"

"Not graveyard. Cemetery."

"There's a difference?"

Yeah. There's a difference."

I stared at Teddy. He didn't look too bad, being deceased and all. Not as bad as some of the other bodies around without their arms or legs knuckles or earlobes. But the eyes were gone, the sockets black and endless, just like all the other corpses.

While I pondered those empty eye holes, Evie stayed back. I could feel her watching me. Guess she knew I must be having a moment.

"So. What *is* the difference?" she said, finally.

I looked at her. "I'm afraid that if you don't know, I can't teach you."

She didn't much care for that, I could tell. We stood there for a few seconds. Each of us waited for the other to say something, but nobody seemed quite ready to do that.

In the distance, I heard a car door creak open and shut, then Gizmo's motor wheezed alive, and it reminded me how sounds travel best on clear, cold nights just like that one. At least that was my theory, anyway.

One more time I cast another glance down at Ted's body, remembering what he said to me in that late night at his house all those years ago.

I looked back up at Evie. "Did you ever wonder why they call this place Whistle Mill?"

"Not really," she said.

"Well, there's a story." I took a breath, working my way into the moment. "On some nights – nights just like tonight - when the weather's just clear enough, when there's no wind rustling the leaves, if you listen just right you can hear the souls of the dead, making their way across the grounds. It's a whistle sound. A long, low whistle. As a matter of fact, I heard it a few minutes ago. Not loud, now. Not loud at all."

Evie started walking again. "Come on, Grady. Let's get out of here." She swung her arm in a big half-circle, motioning me to follow.

Instead, I asked, "Did you hear it?"

"Hear it?"

"The whistle. The dead. Right before we saw them."

She didn't answer immediately, just kept moving towards the sound of Jasper's car. She was thinking about it, though. I could tell that much. And she could think about it all wanted.

She didn't have to say anything at all, as far as I was concerned. I knew she heard the same thing I did - the sound of the dead. That mournful whistle, that shrill signal, long and low from beyond the grave, crying out in the night air. Coming for her, coming for me, coming for Jasper. Coming for all of us.

But she never did say it out loud. Instead the only thing she uttered was a quiet, "Let's go," and then one more wave of her arm for me to follow her.

This time, I did.

The ride back to Evie's house passed without any conversation between the three of us. Not that we needed any talk; each one of us surely knew what the other two were thinking about.

We dropped Evie off at her family's little mint green A-frame, way up Cotton Creek Road, far enough back in the country that there wasn't hardly much road at all. I offered to walk her to the front door, but she said she'd rather go by herself, that she'd see us later. Her Dad met her at the door and from where I sat, he didn't look too thrilled about the whole situation, so I was glad she'd gone by herself. Anyway he had something to say but she wasn't hearing it, just walked on by and into the house. I don't know if she ever told him the whole truth about where she'd been. I doubt he'd have believed her if she did.

From there we went to my house. Jasper crashed on my bedroom floor; there wasn't a lot of conversation between us then, either. But, I did take the opportunity to mention something that had been sticking with me since earlier in the night.

"I saw Uncle Ted tonight," I said, rolling over on my side so he could hear from his spot on the floor. "Right as were leaving. I saw his body. Evie was with me, I didn't want to say anything, but right there he was —"

"I saw him, too."

"You did?"

"Yeah. Sure as shit. When I was headed back to the car."

That took me by surprise. Knocked me back a little, to be honest. Jasper had seen Uncle Ted in the woods, but not said anything about it until now? That seemed like an important discovery to me, and up until then, I'd never known my friend to keep quiet about important discoveries. At least around me.

"Why didn't you tell me before?" I said.

He took a deep breath. Thought about it. I wondered if maybe in all the night's excitement, he got so shell shocked that it just never occurred to him as something he might want to bring it up.

"I walked right past him," he said, finally. "Couldn't have been too long before you saw him yourself. I didn't want to say anything. Just in case you didn't see. Wouldn't want to get you all stirred up over nothing. And with Evie there, I was afraid we'd have to go into the whole story of the banshee and I just don't know if she's ready to hear all that —"

"It's not nothing."

"Seeing Uncle Ted. Jeez, Jasper, I can't believe you wouldn't even mention it –"

"Sorry, Boo." He thought about it some more. "I really am sorry."

I accepted that. "Did you see, his eyes were gone –"

"Of course they were," said Jasper. "He's been dead a few years now. What did you expect, he was gonna look up, just as fine as you please?"

He laughed. I laughed with him. I didn't expect that response, but Jasper knew I didn't expect it. He knew my brain had to be swimming with the fact that I'd just seen my dead uncle's body laid out on the ground in the aftermath of a zombie horde uprising. He was only trying to take my mind off it.

Our laughter trailed off, leaving a warm silence behind it. We sat there for a while.

"Hey, Jasper," I said finally.

"What?"

"That's three for us."

"I 'm not sure what you mean."

"Think about it. That's three. First, the banshee. Now we got dead people after us. And Ethel Stanton, I don't what else you call her but a witch –"

"She ain't no witch."

"What is she, then?"

He thought about it. "I'm not sure."

"Well, I never saw a witch before tonight, but if that old lady you threw in the fire ain't what a witch looks like, I just don't know what to say."

Jasper shrugged, considered it. Nodded. Okay.

"There's something going on around here," I said. "Something in these woods. I ain't quite pegged it yet, and to be honest, I'm wondering why other folks haven't brought it up before now. I mean, hell. Ms. Stanton didn't turn into a witch yesterday. And we know the banshee's been around at least since Uncle Ted was in high school and it got Jace Watkins. But one way or another, something is going on. You can't tell me it's a coincidence, all of them – zombies, a witch, a banshee – being here together. It wouldn't be… I don't know –"

"Logical?"

"Yeah. Logical."

"Well, I don't know." He took a deep breath, blew it out. "But then again, what's logical about *any* of this? Anyway, it's real. That's what matters."

I didn't really agree with my friend – what mattered wasn't just that it was real, it was *why* it was real. Why all of a sudden, two kids faced wickedness that wasn't supposed to exist anywhere but storybooks. That seemed to me to be a hell of a question.

Jasper didn't seem to want to talk about it, though. That much was clear.

Rather than push the issue, I clasped my hands behind my head and looked up at the ceiling. The room got quiet. Too quiet. Normally we would stay up batting philosophical and scientific questions back and forth between us –

time travel, alien life, infinity, all of that – but not that night.

I got out of bed, put *Return of the Jedi* into the VCR. We watched the first few minutes, but both of us were asleep before Luke Skywalker and company took out Jabba the Hutt's sail barge in the endless deserts of Tatooine.

Tired as we were, we still got up early the next morning, in the cold moments before dawn took full hold. The first shades of daylight lent the sky a milky cataract color, while the rest of the world slept still and silent.

Before Mom and Dad woke up, just like we had the night Uncle Ted died, me and Jasper headed back to Martin Holler, hoping like hell we'd find all those bodies before anybody else did. We had no plan as to what we might actually *do* with them, but nevertheless, it seemed like the right thing to do. If some unsuspecting rabbit hunter stumbled on the scene of several hundred corpses piled on top of another in various states of dress and decay, well, there was no telling what would happen.

Nothing good, for sure.

As it turned out, it didn't matter anyway. By the time we returned to the spot, there weren't any bodies at all. No Ethel Marie Stanton, either. No ripped up deer carcass. No nothing. No signs of digging or dragging or burning. No signs of any means of disposal whatsoever. Everything had vanished.

"What do you suppose happened to them?" I asked Jasper. "That's a lot of rotted corpses to disappear without so much as a hint left behind. You don't think they got back up and marched themselves on down the road, do you?"

"No telling," he said. "Down the road, I doubt it. Somebody would have seen that. But deeper into the woods, or back under dirt? Maybe. I don't know. They ain't here now, that's all I can say."

He kicked around at the ground, pondering. I didn't know what he was thinking about, not exactly. I never knew with Jasper. His mind always ran in twenty directions at once. He could be thinking about zombies, he could be thinking about green fire, he could be thinking about the infinite beyond, he could be thinking about the weather or what he might eat for breakfast.

All I cared about was that he not kick up another one of those bodies, or worse.

"What about Ethel Stanton?" I finally said. "Can you believe it?"

"Nowadays, I can believe anything, Boo," Jasper said. "But I don't want to talk about it right now. I'm tired as all hell. Probably best for us that there's nothing here to see now. Let's go home. There'll be plenty of time to talk later."

I couldn't disagree with that. In those days, there seemed an endless run of tomorrows out there for us to use as we pleased and surely, I thought, we could use one or two of them to sort this all out. It certainly wasn't going anywhere in the meantime.

RETURN OF THE BANSHEE

A couple of nights later, I saw the Boone Creek Banshee for the first time since me and Jasper watched her take Uncle Ted, in the summer of nineteen and eight-six. Only now, she wasn't on Boone Creek, floating above the waters with her tattered, translucent gown trailing in the air behind her.

This time, the banshee appeared right outside the bug-flecked glass of my bedroom window. A steady rain fell from the night sky, but she seemed to float in between the raindrops

I was rearranging all of my VHS cassette tapes alphabetically, looking for a missing copy of *The Adventures of Buckaroo Banzai Across the 8th Dimension*, when I happened to glimpse the ghastly visage. The bedroom light was on, burning a beacon in the darkness of Whistle Mill, and that made it feel even more unreal. A person never expects to see an apparition when a bright light burns overhead; we always find comfort in light as our protection against whatever waits in the murky blackness beyond.

And yet there was the banshee. At first it didn't even register, so I turned my head for a full look and that time, it registered plenty. She hung there, suspended in the air, maybe ten feet from the house. Plenty high enough that her black, dead eyes were level with mine as she stared me down.

Immediate, frigid terror tingled up my neck. I had no idea what to do next. Was she coming for me, the same way she came for Teddy? Of course she was. Why else would she be there? I figured that the reason for her visit would come out soon enough. I just wasn't so sure I really *wanted* to know.

I let go of the video cassettes in my hand and stepped towards the window and the apparition beyond.

Those seemed like the longest, slowest steps I ever took in my life.

The whole time, the banshee never moved. She just kept floating in the air, surrounded by the same eerie glow that I'd seen at Boone Creek. Her thin arms hung limp at her side, wispy and pale. And those eyes, fixed on me...

Eventually, I got to the window and lifted it open. A winter wind blew into my bedroom, but I couldn't say how cold it actually was. I was beyond feeling anything at that point.

"What..." I hesitated, choking on the words. "What are you doing here?"

She gave no answer.

"You can't come in," I said.

Maybe the banshee didn't need permission to come get me – this wasn't Dracula, after all – but I damn sure wasn't going to just offer myself up for her. With both hands, I grabbed the window and slammed it shut again. I wanted something in between us. The glass was all I had.

Slowly she drifted towards me. I didn't run. Running wouldn't do any good, I knew that. If she wanted to take me, she would take me and there was nothing I could do to stop her.

The banshee moved on a smooth line, just like she was floating in water, right up to the window. She never opened her mouth or raised her arms, just moved towards me in terrible, inevitable silence.

Then she was right in front of me.

Her ghostly face peered in from just an inch or two from the window glass, but the glass stayed clear. The banshee exhaled no breath. Strings of white hair slipped back and forth in the wind, obscuring just enough of the ghost woman's skeletal features to keep her a mystery, and keep a terrified knot in the bottom of my gut.

All the while, those black eyes fixed on me. Round and black and soulless, empty as the infinite night itself.

Time passed.

Between us.

Through us.

Around us.

I don't know how long we stayed frozen in place like that; Probably only a few seconds but then again it might have been hours for all I know.

Although she had stopped moving, the white gown trailed behind her, still floating, forever floating.

Then,as quickly as she appeared the banshee was gone, floating upward, to the starlit sky.

I stood there, as if shackled to the bedroom floor with medieval irons, and stared out the window. A cold eternity passed before I realized she'd vanished. A moment after *that*, I felt relief wash over me, muted joy that I was still alive. She hadn't taken me. But that relief was only fleeting, followed by the bleak sense that it was only a matter of time before she visited again.

I didn't sleep much that night. Fits and spurts here and there, more restless journeys into unconsciousness than actual soothing repose. Several times I jerked back into the moment and wasn't sure if I was awake or if I wasn't.

During one of those liminal moments, caught between reality and dreams, between the comfort of the known and the terror of the unknown, I thought I heard Uncle Ted's voice. That unmistakable voice.

I lay on my side, facing the wall, and could have sworn he spoke from the general area of my desk. I couldn't quite make out the exact words, but it *was* Uncle Ted speaking and he *was* speaking to *me*.

Finally I rolled over to have a look.

And there he sat.

The moonlight cast a dim glow about the bedroom, but couldn't penetrate some of the deeper shadows. Still, I could make out Teddy's figure propped up straight in my desk chair, turned around so it faced me. He looked restful as all the world, right foot crossed over left knee, each hand gripping one of the chair's wooden arms.

He had on the same clothes he wore the night he died at Boone Creek. The night the banshee got him.

He looked like hell. Like he'd been in the grave for a while and only recently crawled back out, covered in dirt and putrid skin, with worms and maggots squirming all over him. I couldn't help but think about *American Werewolf in London* and the way David's murdered friend Jack keeps appearing to David in a state of decay that gets progressively worse as the movies goes along.

"What do you think you're doing, Grady Claremont?" he said.

I just about wee-weed myself. Sat straight up in bed and managed a timid, "Uncle Ted?"

"Of course it is. Who else would it be?"

"What are you doing here –"

"Visiting," he said. "We haven't visited for a while. I thought you might enjoy that." His lips drew back into the same smile I'd known while he was alive, and he leaned forward from the shadows, into the moonlight that streamed in through the window.

I noticed his eyes were missing. Just like they had been when I looked down and saw him on the ground in Martin Holler –

"You think she's gonna get you, don't you?"

"Who?" I knew what he meant, but didn't want to admit it.

"Who?" He chuckled. "Who. Who do you think? The banshee. The same one that got me.

You think she's coming for you, too, don't you? You always were the smart one in the family, Grady. I bet you know all about that, how banshees are tied to one family, how that one's been going through ours, picking off the men one at a time the same way a kid at the carnival throws baseballs at milk bottles."

This can't be real, I thought to myself.

This is real.

This can't be real.

"Yeah, she's picked us all off, Grady. And now we're down to just one man left on your mama's side of the family. And that's you, my boy. Only you."

I laid back down. Rolled over, towards the wall, away from him, and pulled the blanket over my head so I couldn't hear the dead talk anymore.

He talked anyway.

"You're the last one, nephew of mine," he said. "And sooner or later, she's gonna get you, just like she got me. Just like she got us all. But you're the smart one. You already knew that. You already knew that, didn't you?"

He kept repeating, his dead voice crackling in the dark. *You're the smart one. She's gonna get you. You're the smart one. You already knew. Don't you already know?* The more he talked, the deeper I went under the bedcovers. After a couple of minutes, all I could hear was the sound of my own blood pumping through my head. Maybe Uncle Ted could have reached out and grabbed me, maybe he couldn't have. My only hope was that he wouldn't do it unless we were face to face.

I'd just lie there, turned towards that wall, looking at the underside of that blanket with my own heartbeat thumping in my ears, and let whatever happen, happen. But I wouldn't turn around. I wouldn't face him.

Eventually, though, he stopped talking. I fell back into sleep. Again I dreamed of the banshee. I dreamed of Uncle Ted, and Jasper, too, all of us on Boone Creek, watching a ghost floating above the black water. I dreamed of Homer and Henry, Uncle Ted's two hound dogs, whimpering and whining with their master nowhere to be seen.

When I woke up an hour later, it was dead quiet in the bedroom once more. I stuck my head back out from beneath the blanket, and saw that I was alone.

It would be almost fifty years before I told Jasper about that visit.

PART THREE

SPACE

GRADUATION DAY

Just like the banshee had floated towards my window, me and Jasper floated through the rest of high school, rising silently above everyone else, watching through the glass but never actually tapping on the window. Two whole years went by like that. We didn't mind at all, either.

We stayed in our bubble because we liked it that way. We made acquaintances – mostly other kids that liked the same horror movies and comic books as us – but we never made any other real friends. Sooner or later either people would get bored with us or we'd get bored with them, and that would be that. It wasn't any sort of plan on our part. It was just the way of things.

Evie Fallon didn't hang around us much after the incident with the Lady of the Woods. She tried. Sure she tried. But where our experiences had led me and Jasper to a place of understanding with the infinity around Whistle Mill, Evie's only sent her straight into hiding.

"I'd rather just pretend it's not real," she said to me once. "It'd just be better that way."

I couldn't blame her for that.

Reading *Fangoria* and watching scary movies on the weekend is an escape for most people, a way out of their real world if only for a few hours each day. Those are easy scares, the flip-the-switch-and-then-you're-off-to-bed sort of scares. Staring down the barrels at the real deal like Evie stared down the barrels, first at that demon witch in the woods and then at all those rotting bodies come to life, well, that's a whole different kind of scary. That's real. You don't just turn that off.

Some of us were just better equipped to handle it, I suppose. Like I said, me and Jasper stayed in our bubble. That was our way. That worked for us. Evie Fallon had a different way. I'm not saying that makes her any less of a person, I'm just saying she couldn't handle it like we did. That's all.

Over the next few weeks, Evie changed everything she could about herself. Gone was what we liked about her in the first place – the horror movies, the comic books, the movie magazines. She drifted towards an entirely different crowd, starting out with some of the teachers' kids, the ball players and such. Not that there's anything wrong with that. It was just different.

After Jasper got Gizmo, his attitude about Whistle Mill went south. I chalked it up to the car giving him a sense of freedom, an independence he hadn't known before, and there's probably a lot of truth to that. Once a man takes his first drink of freedom, he soon wants the whole gallon jug.

He got restless. I suppose he looked at everything around him and decided he didn't want any part of it. No sane person could have a serious beef with that, either. For a teenage boy looking down the road at adulthood, Whistle Mill wasn't exactly the Promised Land. We had the Movie Place, of course, had our metal shop and our lawn mower repair place, had the I.G.A. on one end of town and a Sunoco station on the other. But that was about all we had.

What made it worse, around that time – only a few weeks after the banshee came calling at my bedroom window – me and Jasper both noticed that even the little bit Whistle Mill *did* have started a slow slide towards a bad end. I can't say for sure that the two events were related, but the thought did occur to me that an awful lot changed after her visit.

And by "changed," I mean "started on a serious dive straight into the proverbial toilet."

The first indication of the downward turn came when several of the local shop owners pulled their shingles back in and shut down their businesses for good. Not altogether, but one here, one there. Of course, if even one business closes in a little burg like Whistle Mill, that's a serious blow to the local economy. If *most* of them close, that's bound to turn into a full blown economic depression.

Harvey Jason's gas station started the exodus. Me and Jasper just happened to drive by as Harvey watched the crew pull down that blue and yellow Sunoco sign from his otherwise nondescript concrete building at the end of Maple Street.

That wasn't a huge surprise by itself. After all, in small towns across America, gas stations change ownership hands about as often as conspiracy theorists change tinfoil hats. What we knew as a Sunoco station had been a Texaco once and a Gulf station before that. It wasn't anything new.

So, we waited for the new owners to put their name on the door and get the place back in business. Only this time, no new owners ever came to the rescue. The Sunoco emptied out, and stayed empty. Just a few months after Harvey closed the place down, the weeds took over. We did note the loss, but to be honest it didn't really break our hearts. There were plenty of other gas stations in the county – seventy-something in Sewardville alone.

In the spring of that same year, though, we got some *real* bad news. The Mountain View Drive-in Theater in Sewardville would not open for its summer season that year.

Our only outlet for first-run movies was gone, victim to the economic and technological realities that killed most of the other drive-ins across the U.S.A. following their heyday in the nineteen fifties and sixties. It died and we weren't able to give it a decent burial. At least they gave it a front page story in the Sewardville *Times*.

Junior year, the colleges started to come calling. ACT scores, SAT scores, that sort of thing. Apparently me and Jasper weren't as dumb as Ethel Stanton thought. Neither one of us wanted to think about it but we knew that we'd have to make some decisions sooner or later.

On occasion, we'd have conversations about our future that usually went something like:

"Where do you want to go to college, Jasper?"

"I don't know exactly, but I can tell you one thing: wherever it is, it'll be somewhere – anywhere – far from Whistle Mill, Kentucky. California seems nice. Alaska. Hawaii, maybe. And if I can find a place that's further away than that I'll see if they have a college there, too."

"You'll have to speak Russian or Chinese."

"I might."

"You will."

"Well if it comes to it, I can learn Russian. I can by-hell learn Chinese."

"What about Korean?"

"Korean, too. If that's what it takes to get out of here, sign me up."

But while Jasper was thinking about foreign languages, I was trying to figure out if I wanted to go to college at all.

On the surface, higher education didn't appeal to me. Throughout most of my school life, I'd assumed that after high school I'd move on to the university like a good little boy, but by the time I could actually see that step on the horizon, suddenly it didn't seem quite so appealing. Hardly an automatic.

By that point it was clear that I'd had enough of school. I wanted to put the books down for a while. Maybe Mom and Dad had other plans, but they weren't the ones doing all the homework. I didn't know exactly what I wanted with the next few years of my life, but I was pretty certain it didn't involve research papers and student loans.

The thought nagged me. Over the next few months it became more than a nag. Maybe Jasper was ready to run off to college, but the more I thought about it the more I realized that I needed a break from the books. I could always go back later.

The other big shift we noticed around Whistle Mill during our last couple years of high school was more insidious in nature.

The local criminal element.

Of all the changes happening around me, the creeping increase of crime in Seward County probably unnerved me more than anything. I could handle banshees, witches, the living dead – anything of the sort that crossed my path. But drug dealers? Prostitutes? Home invaders and car thieves? Now *that* sort of thing made my skin crawl.

Seward County had always been home to your basic rabble rousers. Your long hairs, driving around in their Chevy S-10 pickup trucks, booming Lynnyrd Skynnyrd ("Freebird," natch) and Tom Petty ("American Girl", natch) out of their speakers, carrying a joint in the ashtray and a Styrofoam cooler full of Bud Light cans in the passenger's side floorboard, underneath a blanket or whatever. (Because of course the sheriff's deputies wouldn't think to look under *there*.). Those folks didn't bother me. I guess they just always seemed like a natural part of rural American life.

But drug dealers?

Prostitutes?

Come on.

I mean, you have got a town of four hundred people, a whole county of maybe ten thousand, and there are *prostitutes* walking the streets? Straight up, no hiding, even-the-police-are-aware prostitutes.

Once, I overheard Mom and Dad discuss the fact that if you saw one of the prostitutes walking around with an open cup in her hand, that meant she was open for business. "Available." A closed cup meant she was open but unavailable, so check back later.

What kind of town do you live in where people actually have that sort of conversation? And how in the *hell* did my parents know *anything* about the details of local prostitute commerce?

We all supposed – well, me and Jasper supposed, anyway – that the trash drifted over to Whistle Mill from the other end of the county. Sewardville claimed an inordinate number of toughs and would-be gangsters among its population. Rumor was that the whole Sheriff's department was in on it, taking donations under the table from a couple of young gun Don Corleone godfather wannabes. Supposedly they were all using the Faulkner Funeral Home as their clearinghouse, burning up evidence and bodies in the cremation furnace late at nights when the law-abiding citizenry was deep into R.E.M. sleep.

It all made sense to me, too, in that creepy sort of small town, *Dead and Buried* kind of way. Of course, I doubted Harley Faulkner was capable of resurrecting the deceased like the town doctor did in that movie, but then again, given what we'd seen up to that point, you couldn't rule anything out.

The great Whistle Mill crime wave started small, as the yahoos from Sewardville spread their influence down Highway 15. We heard about a few little events, but nothing that turned your head too much: a broken garage window here, busted mailbox there, maybe the occasional shoplifter down at the IGA.

But it got worse.

One day at lunch during our senior year of high school, Jasper picked out his college: Stanford University.

"Why Stanford?" I asked him. That seemed like a perfectly reasonable question between to friends from Eastern Kentucky.

"Stanford? Like, California Stanford?"

"Yeah."

"Why?"

"Because I got in, that's why."

Fair enough.

*

Somewhere in there, meth came to town. I'm not exactly sure when. All I know is, it happened. As my Granny Claremont used to say, Oh my goodness gracious, did it ever happen.

If you don't know much about meth, count yourself lucky. Personally, I've never been within five hundred yards of it myself – not knowingly, anyway. But I've seen the drug do enough damage that if I could stay five *thousand* yards away from it, I'd do that.

Five thousand yards is an awful long distance in a place like Seward County, though.

Once meth got hold in Whistle Mill, it was there to stay. The rabble rousers found it and got hooked. The prostitutes found it, and got hooked. Some Moms and Dads found it, and they got hooked. Anybody that touched meth turned their life over to it just as easy as turning a nickel over to a gumball machine.

I couldn't understand it. Jasper couldn't understand it. We couldn't understand it. If you've ever seen a person on meth, you don't understand it, either.

Meth rots human beings from the inside out. It tears holes in their skin, turns teeth into nubby charcoal bits, makes the eyes sour yellow. It makes people into monsters. Devours bodies and shits out souls, that's what meth does. Every time I saw someone on the street who'd been on the stuff – and it was easy enough to tell one who had from one who hadn't – I thought about those rotten corpses crawling along the ground back at Martin Holler.

I wondered if maybe these new monsters walking around the Mill were Ethel Stanton's of finally getting back at us for tossing her in the flames that frosty December night.

It was in those years that I realized for the first time just how badly people can treat themselves. Smoking a little reefer's not enough. Not pills or cocaine, either. Those habits get expensive. No. I saw it for myself, that there were people in the world who wanted to get high so damn bad, that they'd put chemicals in their bodies you wouldn't put in a junk car engine. Get out a little Drano, some window cleaner, bust up some light bulb filaments, grind in a little steel wool, then douse the pile with paint thinner, mix everything together and have right at it. Smoke it, snort it, shoot it up.

I even heard of some people injecting it straight up their own rectums. *They wanted to get high so bad that they shot household chemicals right up their own asses.* Sounds awful. Is awful. But I surely did hear that.

Want to know what people in this world will to do get high? Jasper told me once that he'd heard – and I don't have any reason not to believe him – that after people eventually burned themselves out on cleaning supplies, they'd take to storing their own piss and shit in plastic buckets for months at a time, and they'd actually use *that* to trip into the starry, starry night.

You heard right.

After a few months, once those ingredients sat around and got good and ripe, they'd mix them together into a frothy stew and party down. Smoke it, snort it, shoot it up. Actually, I don't know how they took this particular caramel delight, but does it really matter? We're talking about people who can't get high enough off your garden variety opiates to suit themselves. Can't get a good buzz from whatever irradiated chemicals might be under the bathroom sink. No, hell no. But fish-lippin' dingleberry remnants? Bring that right the hell on!

Anyway, the place was in decline. That's all I'm saying.

After all the gas-huffers from Sewardville expanded their shady empire across the county into Whistle Mill, it didn't take long before the scuzzier elements of the community got bored with just getting high, breaking windows, and shoplifting beer. Pills got popular. Vandalism, too. Somebody painted "666" on every stop sign in town, which I actually thought was kind of funny but which caused quite a kerfuffle among a few of the old ladies around town, seeing as they were all proud former Reaganistas. I guess they thought maybe the devil worshippers had come back to claim the blonde haired and blue eyed kids they missed the first time around.

The worse it got, the more you'd see prostitutes out and about. Probably they were just looking to make a few quick bucks to support their own drug habits, but I did wonder if there might also be a weird plot afoot whereby the prostitutes weren't prostitutes at all, but androids, half robot and half woman monsters. Sort of like a skankier Stepford wives, as if their mad scientist creator was setting up an army to overtake us all.

I started seeing the same girl wandering the streets at all hours. Maybe she staked out her territory. She strutted around way too close to the Movie Place for my comfort, I'll say that. I took this personally, like whatever crabs or skin crawlies she might be carrying would somehow get transmitted into Bobby's store and from there, onto me. It didn't help that every time I saw the girl, her whore's cup always had a lid on it. "Check back later." I was never quite sure if that meant she was on her way to a rendezvous with romance, or leaving one.

So the prostitutes were pretty bad. The meth heads weren't great, either. But when it was all said and done, if you asked me what wound up the single worst scourge to hit my hometown of Whistle Mill during the years when I was finishing up high school, my vote would go to the pill heads. No question.

I can't pinpoint exactly when painkillers became such a widespread problem, and it really wasn't until the turn of the twenty-first century that the problem fully exploded on our corner of the world. But a few years before that, during our senior year, me and Jasper started overhearing conversations in the hallways of the high school that went something like:

"Hey, you going to that party up at Steph's house Saturday?"

"Sure. You?"

"Yeah, I'm going."

"Cool."

"Cool."

"I heard Raleigh Peak was gonna be up there, too."

"Really?"

"Really."

"You think he might have some Xannies?"

"Sure. Dude's always got Xannies. Probably some Vikes, too, if you like those better."

"Cool."

"Cool."

"Those Xannies'll get you totally wild, dude."

"Totally."

"Cool."

Yeah. Cool. Totally cool."

Now, the two of us weren't educated enough at the time to know that Xannies meant Xanax and Vikes meant Vicodin. Maybe you are, but we weren't. We preferred to keep our heads in the sand when it came to that sort of business. We had banshees, demons, and other worlds to worry about. Still, you can't help but hear a conversation like that without knowing the people talking aren't out for wholesome family fun. And the more you hear that conversation, the more you start to realize, *this is kind of messed up.*

Kids brought little yellow and red pills to English class, wrapped in sandwich bags, shoved into the purses and the pockets of their Seward

County High letter jackets. On occasion one guy or another would offer me or Jasper some of that gnarly medicine, but we would just kind of smirk and shake our heads. Looking back on it I think they just offered to be polite. They knew we'd never take them up on it and to be perfectly honest I doubt they'd behave made the offer at all if they thought there was any chance we'd accept. After all, anything we got would have come out of their stash. Not happening.

The pills were bad enough by themselves. Teenagers eating pharmaceuticals like pop rock candy, walking the hallways with glassy eyes, letting their ambitions dissipate into the ether and not caring about it all. Not a good scene at all. There's a certain sadness in witnessing decent people flush themselves straight down the grand ole toilet bowl of life, you know?

But even worse than all those pills were the shenanigans that came to town along with them.

Nobody turns into a thief faster than a pillhead.

Don't ask me why. Meth ingredients are cheap, maybe that's it, I don't know. All I can tell you is, if a person needs to scrape together a few dollars for a Lortab or a Xanax or heaven forbid an OxyContin, the last thing that pill popper's gonna is do is go out and work for their money. Unless you consider robbery, assault, or breaking and entering to be "work," in which case if you do, we can't be friends anymore.

*

We couldn't escape the feeling that Whistle Mill was crumbling around us. Eventually we just accepted it. It didn't matter that much, anyway; Jasper was headed off to Stanford, and I was headed... somewhere. I wasn't quite sure *where* just yet, but somewhere.

June of the year nineteen and ninety-three marked the end of our time in the Seward County public school system.

Graduation Day arrived, on a Sunday in the fuzzy summer heat of the Seward High gymnasium. The class valedictorian gave a speech, as did the salutatorian and a couple of older folks we didn't recognize. Doctors or lawyers, maybe. Whatever.

After they were all through talking, me and Jasper and the rest of the seniors walked across the stage, got our diplomas and shook hands with the Superintendent. Then we were done. I can't say we learned a whole lot in K through twelve, not from the school system, at least. If I haven't exactly spent a lot of time describing in great detail our adventures in academics, that's because there isn't much adventure to report on that front. But we got through.

Later that night, one of the basketball players threw a graduation party at his family's farm.

To our surprise, Evie Fallon invited us to go with her, even though we'd barely spoken since that whole incident with the Lady of the Woods. We thanked her for the invite, politely refused, and headed to the Movie Place instead. Little did we know, we'd end up at that party regardless.

ME AND JASPER AND THE LITTLE RED PILLS

Before we get into the story of what happened at the big graduation soiree, let's talk a little bit about family.

In places like Whistle Mill, which aren't exactly population dense, there tends to be just a few families that dominate the social scene over all the rest. Generally what happens is one member of the family comes into some money or land through means that might or might not be legitimate, then that money stays in the family and grows through following generations. Kind of like termites – once that cash gets into the family tree, it ain't coming out unless you burn it out.

In the Seward County of my younger days, two families ran the whole shooting match. The Slones had the Sewardville end. Me and Jasper went to school with John Slone. Back then his daddy was already making a name for himself in that scuzzy, underworld sort of way. Pills, meth, gambling, that sort of thing. John ended up Sheriff and a few years after that he ended up dead. Eventually his sister took over the family business and kept the money rolling in.

On the Whistle Mill end of the county, the Peak family were the ones with their hands in everything, at least that's how it seemed, the way everybody whispered their names and got all hunched up in the back anytime that family came up in discussion.

Curious thing about the Peaks, however. They weren't seen around too often. Hardly ever. Mostly they stayed up on Goforth Mountain, in their creaky old farmhouse which was big as any five other houses in Whistle Mill and probably a hundred years older, too. They didn't have any notable business interests. Never showed any interest in politics, either. But somehow, their money never ran out. And their family name lived on in whispers of those that lived in their shadow.

On occasion the Peaks threw a party. They'd invite a lot of people from out of town, and the next day some interesting details would make the gossip rounds. I was never lucky enough to attend one of those parties, but I do know a few people who did, and they all told the same stories about just how big and old that house really is. A man could stand in one corner of the gigantic living room, they said, and not see anything but shadows in the opposite corner side as the floor stretched away into darkness.

They swore up and down they saw a thousand people or more in that at one time, too. They really did say that. I didn't have any reason not to believe them.

But even the people who went up to that huge house on Goforth Mountain couldn't tell you where the Peak family fortune came from. Oh sure, they could tell you there was plenty of it to go around – after all, it took a lot of funds to run an estate of that size, let alone throw the kinds of parties that they threw up there. But they couldn't say where the money came from.

But me and Jasper, we found out.

We found out the night Evie Fallon called us to her friend's high school graduation party.

We'd turned her down at first, and instead headed to the Movie Place then back to my house to watch a quadrupleheader of David Cronenberg's *Scanners, Videodrome, The Dead Zone,* and *The Fly* as our last hurrah to high school. We got most of the way through it, too, when shortly after midnight, my telephone rang during the scene in *The Fly* where Seth Brundle is upside-down on the ceiling, showing Veronica his new wall walking skills.

I have to be honest here. That's one of my favorite scenes in the movie and I didn't really want to get up and answer the phone in the middle of it. So, I let it ring.

"You gotta answer," Grady said.

"Why? I'm watching this."

"Nobody calls in the middle of the night unless it's something important."

He was right. So, I answered.

"Hello?"

"Hello? Grady?" I recognized Evie's voice immediately. But now, her voice sounded shaky. Scared, even.

"Evie?"

"Do you have Jasper there with you?"

"Yeah, he's here. Why?"

She took a deep breath, and as she inhaled I could hear the air quiver through her lips. "Grady, I know we haven't talked much in the last couple of years," she said, "and I know you don't want to come to this party. But there's something going on up here. I don't know what it is. Just something. I think it'd be good if you and Jasper got here soon. I'm afraid we might... need you."

Now, under normal circumstances, me and Jasper would never have attended such a gathering. Like I told you before, we preferred operating in the margins. Parties with ball players and cool kids just weren't our style. Not even if Evie was the one inviting us. And hell, she said herself that we'd barely talked to each other in the long months since that horrible incident at Martin Holler.

But the way Evie sounded on the phone made me think that maybe we ought to see what she meant. She had the same jittery tone in her voice that she did the night we stumbled through the darkness, running from dead people. I'm not usually the sentimental type, but that told me we'd be going against our better natures if we didn't check it out.

So, me and Jasper turned off *The Fly* and headed outside quiet so as not to wake up my Mom and Dad. Then we got into Gizmo and drove away to find Evie.

The party took place in a barn behind the house of a kid named Scotty Davenport. He doesn't really play into this story but I'm telling you just for the sake of accuracy.

We had a decent idea of where Scotty lived, but as we got close we started seeing cars and pickup trucks parked on the side of the road. Not far after that the vehicles spread into the surrounding fields and finally a spacious yard in front of an old white farmhouse. In places like Seward County, that type of parking arrangement is usually a dead giveaway that there's a party nearby.

We followed the trail of cars up to the house then drove around and parked in the rear, about fifty yards away from the barn.

As we opened Gizmo's doors and exited the vehicle, the sound of generic country music blasted across the grounds. Way too loud for my tastes. Garth Brooks, George Strait, Alan Jackson. To be honest, I didn't much know the difference between one and the other.

From what I could tell, the house was in good shape but barn, not so good. It wasn't quite run down all the way yet, but it would be before too long. Weeds snaked up the outside of the walls, headed towards a rooftop that already showed a slight sag towards the center.

Four sets of generator-powered light banks created a wide halo of artificial daylight around the structure and partially inside it, throwing long shadows of teenagers against the faded grey wood.

From where we stood, the place looked full, wall to wall. Some of the kids danced, some staggered drunk and tried not to fall down or puke. A few even succeeded.

I recognized a good number of the revelers as classmates who had walked across the stage and gotten their diplomas earlier that day, same as me and Jasper.

That didn't apply to everyone, of course. A good party attracts all sorts. Some older folks walked about in small clusters, guys and gals in their twenties doing all they could to hang onto the ghosts of high school years past. Other people that I recognized as younger than me slunk around the edges of the gathering, juniors and sophomores and even a stray freshman or two, sipping from plastic cups, practicing for the celebrations they imagined must be waiting for them in their own glorious futures.

Near one of the barn's rear corners, in the inky area where the elevated lights barely reached, I saw what looked like a man and woman kissing. When the man glanced over and made eye contact with me, I realized it was Raleigh Peak, the youngest of the Peak sons, and Evie Fallon. And they weren't kissing, either. Matter of fact it looked like she was trying to push him the hell off her.

Now, I knew Raleigh Peak. Not personally, but I knew who he was. Everybody in Whistle Mill did, just like they knew all the members of his family. But this was the first time I ever came within ten yards of him.

Raleigh looked to me like he was around twenty-five or six years old. For a bunch of high school kids, being halfway to thirty meant he possessed copious amounts of knowledge and experience from innumerable trips to the outer reaches of the vast Milky Way, if not even beyond them. He wore loose blue jeans and a short-sleeved Hawaiian shirt over top of a crisp white tank top. The Hawaiian shirt lay unbuttoned and open wide, its garish yellow, blue, and orange flowers screaming out like anguished souls lost in the abyss.

His skin was smooth and shiny, the color of desert sand. Dark sunglasses sat perched atop his blonde buzzcut hair. He smiled. A lot.

Despite all his attempts at charming her into submission, Evie appeared utterly offended by Raleigh Peak's mere presence. When he tried to get closer to her, she couldn't hide her irritation, and pushed him away.

I could have sworn that even over the country music blaring around us, I heard her say, "Get away from me!"

"Hey!" I yelled at them. "You okay, Evie?"

She didn't say anything, just looked towards the ground.

I walked in their direction, with Jasper right behind me. The whole way, Raleigh never moved, never stopped looking at me.

"What can I do for you boys?" Raleigh said, smiling at us as we strolled to a stop three feet from where he stood with Evie. She looked at us, then at him, then back at us again.

"Evie? You okay?" I asked her.

She came over where me and Jasper stood.

"She's fine," Raleigh said without a trace of good humor. "I hope the two of y'all boys didn't come here to start trouble."

"That depends," said Jasper.

"Depends on what?"

"Depends on which way you want this to go, I guess."

Jasper tensed up – I could see the cords tighten in his neck from where I was standing – and the thought occurred to me that somebody was about to get hit. It was fifty-fifty Peak or Bohanon, but one or the other for sure.

This was a side of Jasper I hadn't seen before. We'd always laid back around most folks, treat social situations with a big ol' dose of sly sarcasm. Now he was poised to throw a haymaker to protect a lady's honor? A lady he'd barely even talked to for the last two years? Maybe Raleigh Peak was just the one guy to hit Jasper's ornery nerve.

After he thought about it for a second, Raleigh threw back his head and let out a booming laugh that seemed about as sincere as a three dollar bill. "Okay, then. I gotcha," he said. "You want it *that* way. Fine. It can go that way. If it's alright with you, I'd just as soon go in here and enjoy the festivities."

He laughed again, seemed impressed with himself. We didn't find anything funny, though, and as Raleigh realized that we weren't in on the joke, the grin slid off his face. He took on the hard facial expression of barely-contained aggression.

We didn't give any ground.

Then, Raleigh's stormy visage broke. Just like that. He walked away towards the barn, mumbling to himself as he went. I couldn't make out the words exactly, but the tone was clear enough. I had a feeling he planned to see us again soon.

Funny thing about it was, once we got away from the asshole, Evie decided she didn't want to leave the party, after all. I found that confusing, seeing as how she'd been uncomfortable enough to call us for help with Raleigh Peak and he hadn't really gone anywhere but a few yards around the corner.

As soon as he was out of her face, though, Evie's mood flip-flopped and she seemed ready to enjoy herself again.

"I wanna go back in. You guys come with me," she said.

Me and Jasper looked at her like she'd just told us to cut our own heads off.

"Come on," she continued. "It's been a while. Who knows how many more chances we'll have after tonight, now that school's out for good?"

Before I could turn down the offer – and I wanted to turn it down, believe you me – Jasper intervened.

"Okay. Let's do it," he declared without anywhere near what I considered an appropriate amount of consideration. "Last night of high school. We're in."

A series of spiteful curses ran through my mind, but I kept them quiet while my eyes glared straight at Jasper, making sure he knew I wasn't thrilled about this turn of events. I'd come up here to help Evie and get the hell out as soon as we were done. Oh well.

He only offered a mischievous wink back.

"All right, then." I said to Evie. "I guess we're goin'."

She linked arms with us, and headed towards the barn's entrance. Nobody said anything the first few steps, but I could tell by the way Evie's jaw fidgeted from side to side that she was chewing on some words and it was only a matter of time before they worked their way out in conversation.

Five seconds later...

"Thank you guys for coming to get me," she said. "I'm sorry this was so out of the blue, I just didn't know who else to call."

"Don't worry about it," said Jasper.

"Did you think we wouldn't come?" I asked.

"Nah. Not really." Evie's voice trailed off. She faced straight ahead, but kept talking to us. "It's just... all that... stuff. Just stuff. You know. Dead people comin' alive. A friggin' witch. I didn't know what to say about it. What can you say about it? I didn't know to say."

Jasper nodded. "Did you ever try talking to anybody else? Anybody besides us?"

"No, hell no. Uh-uh," Evie giggled. "How do you tell a story like that and not get carted off to the crazy house?"

For one reason or another, that rubbed me the wrong way. "You could have talked to us about it, you know."

She looked over at me. "I could have. Sure. But I didn't, and I'm sorry. Guess I just needed to work through it myself. What can I say?"

Jasper took a breath, let it out long and slow. "You can't say anything. Because when you get right down to it, there's nothing much to say."

We arrived at the barn door, which was wide open. I could see inside that the barn was filled with folks I recognized from our class and even more folks that I didn't. Revelers, rabble rousers, no telling what else.

Evie didn't even stop. She just went right on in there like she owned the place. After a brief hesitation, me and Jasper followed.

Crossing through that door gave me the distinct impression of traversing a barrier into an otherworldly plane of noisy, almost psychedelic existence.

It reminded me of a John Hughes movie set in a country & western bar.

Strings of forty-watt light bulbs hung from the rafters in loose arcs, starting in the corners of the ceiling and running in to a disconnected fan that served as their central hub. Farm implements hung about with no particular sense of order – rakes, shovels, machetes, a pitchfork, a chainsaw, several other vaguely weapon-like items that I didn't recognize thanks to my utter lack of farm knowledge. Loose straw covered the dirt floor, thin in the middle of the floor but more clumped together as it ran against the walls. Dust particles and summer bugs danced together in the artificial light, unnoticed by the partiers except when they flew to close to an uncovered cup of beer.

Near the entrance, a couple of beer kegs sat on the ground in red plastic tubs full of ice. In the corner behind the door, three guys played a Garth Brooks song on their guitars, serenading anybody who cared to listen and the rest of us who didn't.

Just as we entered the room, a couple of scruffy guys that none of us recognized started shoving each other. The party hit the pause button, and everybody turned to watch with mild curiosity. One of the pair – a short guy, maybe five foot six, in denim shorts and a Duck Head t-shirt – took a drunken swing at the other, who was at least six inches taller and forty pounds heavier, and who had on a green army jacket even though it was at least ninety in the barn. The short guy's swing went wild, missed by at least a foot, and he lost his balance and landed on his shoulder. The dude in the army jacket just shook his head. Everybody else had a laugh, then went about their business.

By that time, I was already trying to come up with a graceful exit. This was not my sort of place. It did not exist inside our preferred bubble.

Then I saw Raleigh Peak again.

He stood in the corner farthest from the door, a good thirty or forty feet away, back in the nether reaches of the barn where light from the strings of bulbs hanging overhead began its long dissolve into the shadows.

His back was to us, but those sunglasses on top of his head gave him away.

He'd cornered a couple of guys that I recognized from the basketball team – Ben Colan and Jason Kirby, both of them tall and wiry and dumber than owl shit as far as anybody ever could tell – and was regaling them with some story or another. Between the music and the general din of a lot of people in a small space, I couldn't hear anything he said to them but it sure looked like he was having a good time saying it.

Ben and Jason looked like they were having a good time listening, too. While Raleigh talked, they both held the exact same pose: arms crossed, head craned forward, eyes squinted. They kept nodding, too, as though this young man just a few years their senior dispensed the most important, life-changing advice they could ever hope to hear. They were Bounty paper towels, soaking it all up.

They had on their varsity letter jackets, too, which I found hilarious because a) it was June and not exactly jacket weather, and b) I always thought people looked hilarious when they wore their letter jackets outside of school.

I watched them for a minute. Raleigh talking, Ben and Jason enrapt. Then, Raleigh reached into his pocket, pulled something out, and handed it to Ben. At first I couldn't tell what it was – it didn't look like much more than a fast handshake – but when Ben held the little object up towards what dim light shone into their corner of the barn, I finally saw it.

A pill bottle.

Just your common, everyday pill bottle. Translucent orange-brown plastic, topped by a white childproof lid. Millions of them the world over.

Ben eyed the bottle, and once satisfied that it had contained whatever he thought it was supposed to contain, tossed it over to Jason, who shoved it into the pocket of his letter jacket and glanced around just to make sure nobody was paying any attention to them.

He actually made eye contact with me for just the briefest moment, but I suppose he didn't consider us important enough to bother with.

As Jason wandered away, Ben pulled out a wad of cash and gave it to Raleigh. At least he tried to give it to him. But Raleigh just held up one hand, smiled, and refused to take the money. He motioned with his head that they should all head back outside.

On their way out the door, the group passed within a couple feet of me, Jasper, and Evie. We tried our best to give off the impression that we couldn't care less whether they were coming or going.

Raleigh, on the other hand, did his best to come off like a complete asshole, brushing me with his shoulder as he went past us.

"That boy ain't right," said Grady.

"Nah," I said, "he ain't."

After they left, we wandered around the party for a while.

Eventually, a kid wandered up to me with his hand wrapped around a mostly full fifth of Jack Daniels Tennessee whiskey. He had curly black hair, black as a rat's eyes. He was tall, a good six-three, and muscular, especially in the shoulders and forearms. He wore dark gray sweatpants, with an AC/DC *Highway to Hell* t-shirt that featured Angus Young proudly displaying his devil's horns and tail.

From the way he smelled, and the way he couldn't walk a straight line to save his own life, I guessed he'd finished that first half of the bottle all by himself.

"Hey. I know you," he said. He locked his gaze on me, but never smiled.

"Well, I don't know you," I replied.

I looked at Jasper. He didn't know this guy. Same with Evie.

"I do know you, though," the kid went on, unfazed, as If he'd heard me thinking about him. "You're Grady Claremont. You're the one whose uncle got killed a few years ago, up Boone Creek."

Wow. Straight to the big topics.

"Yeah, that's me. That was my Uncle Ted," I managed, hoping the rest of the conversation would just sort of float away.

It seemed liked the kid sensed that I didn't care to follow that line of question. He cut himself off, and held his whiskey up.

"To your Uncle Ted, then."

"Thanks, but no thanks," I said.

Not only had I never had a drink in my life, I'd never even been within three feet of one until that moment. I didn't have anything against adult beverages – I wasn't Ethel Stanton, I didn't think liquor was the devil's urine and teenagers were his toilet bowl – but I didn't have any interest in it, either. I'd seen enough adults throw back a few too many and blow dinner chunks in Uncle Ted's backyard that the fun of alcohol was lost on me.

The kid offered once more. "What's the matter Never had a drink before?"

"What's your name, anyway?" I asked. "I don't think I've ever seen you around –"

"Randall," he said. "My name's Randall. Not that it matters at this point."

"Randall who?"

"Don't worry about it," he said. "Like I told you, my name don't matter anyway. Hell, I've got lots of names. More names than I know what to do with. I'm just Randall tonight. I might be somebody different tomorrow. Who knows? It don't matter. But what *does* matter is, you're a grown up now. Think about it, man. You're gonna be an old man soon enough. Might as well get a little burn in your belly." He held up the bottle again. "Come on. To Uncle Ted."

I shook my head. "Nah, I'm good. Really."

I looked at the whiskey.

I glanced at Jasper.

Images of Uncle Ted flashed in my brain. Telling stores in his concrete block building. Sitting on his couch, watching horror movies in the darkness. Running through the woods of Boone Creek. His body lying on the ground in Martin Holler, dead, resurrected, then dead again.

"All right," I said to Randall, and took the bottle. "Let's do it then. To Uncle Ted"

I took a hard pull on the Jack Daniels, and heard Jasper say something to Evie underneath his breath that sounded like, "Oh hell. This ought to be good."

The whiskey, it burned. Oh, did it ever burn. Lit me up bigger than a Chinese dynamite factory if you want to know the truth of the matter – threw fire in my eyes and stars in my belly. Made me think of gasoline mixed with battery acid. There were a couple ticks of the clock where I thought for sure I'd projectile vomit at a Linda-Blair-in-*The-Exorcist* level, but somehow I beat that back.

Then I grabbed Randall's bottle, and slammed back another mighty drink.

Then another.

And another.

It goes like that when a man takes the first drink of his life and doesn't get immediately shit hammered drunk. He thinks, "No big deal. I can do this." When that first dink doesn't set the room a-spinning, a sort of comfort settles in. *No big deal. I can do this.* The rookie drinker puffs out his chest, asks for another shot of liquor, downs that one, too, which of course doesn't have any more immediate effect on sobriety than the first one did. So he drinks another. And another. And another, and another, wham wham wham, quick as he can, as many anothers as it takes until the bottle's empty. Then he finds another bottle.

And I found another bottle.

At any high school graduation party, half-filled bottles of cheap liquor are bound to be common as cancer. Reckon I managed to get my hands around just about every one laying around that particular party, too. Tvarscki vodka, hundred proof. Beefeater gin. Kessler whiskey (blended – "smooth as silk"). El Toro tequila. The swill. Even snuck in a couple of Milwaukee's Best, too, which everybody knows is pretty much the bottom of the barrel when it comes to beer. Nobody drinks Milwaukee's best unless they're already drilled out of their minds. Trust me. I know.

I didn't drink every bottle dry but I got a good tug off more than a few. Eventually – I couldn't say how long since at a certain point I lost all concept of time and space – my piss-poor decisions started catching up with me.

Someone once told me that alcohol is a creeper drug, that it comes up on you from behind and knocks you flat on your ass without so much as ringing your doorbell first. I don't know if I agree with that, though. In my experience, alcohol is much more of a rising flood. Sobriety is your flood wall. You can drink and drink and drink with little if any effect, but all that time you're drinking, the flood builds in your body. Sobriety might hold everything at bay for a while, but eventually, the waters are gonna rise high enough that they're going over top of that wall. And when they do, it's one hellacious mess, and by that time, you're in way too bad of a shape to deal with it.

That's what happened to me in that barn on the first night I ever got drunk. The wall broke and the flood crashed in. One minute I was fine, the next minute my face got hot and the room went to swimming. I took a couple of steps and felt myself sway side to side like a rubber ducky in a bathtub.

The next thing I knew, Evie wrapped her arms around my waist from behind, a valiant but ultimately futile effort to keep me from falling flat on my face. I heard Jasper say, "Hold on there, big fella," right before I went down. And the world skidded to a stop, and everything went black.

I woke up outside, curled up in the back of a white Chevy S10 pickup truck, my arms tucked under me just like a sleeping toddler. The swimmy feeling in my head hadn't gone away, but it was dulled just enough that I could focus my eyes a little and see the stars overhead. It wasn't too long after I'd passed out, judging by the sounds emanating from the barn that suggested the party still rolled on at full strength.

I sat up and looked around, but couldn't see anybody. As soon as I got vertical, though, I felt something traveling up my belly, into my throat, and knew it was serious trouble. My head barely got over the edge before the puke sprayed out.

Mid-vomit, I heard a familiar voice.

"Welcome back to the world," Jasper said. He sat by himself on the ground, back rested against the rear driver's side wheel of the truck. I'd missed throwing up on his head by maybe two feet. He appeared unfazed.

"I ain't back yet," I said collapsing into the truck bed.

While I laid there in the bed, Jasper stood up. He pulled the truck's tailgate down and sat on it by himself. For the next few minutes, as he talked he never turned around and looked at me. Just kept staring up at the sky. He did that a lot when he was deep in thought, talking to me without actually looking at me. I always figured it was easier for him to handle two things at once if he only made eye contact with one of them. If his eyes and mouth could work on different thoughts at the same time.

"Where's Evie?" I asked.

"She took off with one of the guitar player. It's just you and me again, dude."

He laughed. I didn't find it all that funny.

"You mean, we came all the way up here just to help her, and now that she's been helped, she doesn't even stick around to say 'thanks'? What's that all about?"

"Give her a break," he said. "She's had a rough night. We'll see her again sooner or later. Besides, she came out here to check on you but you were dead trashed at that point. So don't get too high and mighty about it."

"I'm not."

"You are."

"You're covering for her."

"You're being high and mighty."

"I'm not being high and mighty."

I didn't want to talk about it anymore.

I closed my eyes, squeezed my head with one hand hard as I could. My vision steadied for a moment and pushed the slosh back down into my stomach.

"How long was I out, anyway?" I asked him. Even though I could hear the party hadn't slowed down, and knew that in terms of real time not much had gone by since I crashed and burned in the barn, I still felt like I'd woken up in a different geologic area. Passed out drunk in the Mesozoic, woke up slightly less drunk in the Cenozoic. Something like that.

"About ten minutes," said Jasper.

"Ten minutes?" He had to be kidding,

"Nah man, that's it. You hit the ground pretty hard. Must have knocked yourself a couple steps back towards sobriety."

I opened my eyes again but stayed down right there in the truck bed, listening to the sound of blood as it pumped through my head. I hoped like hell that it would eventually circulate the vodka/gin/tequila/whiskey/beer cocktail out of my body but I couldn't be certain about that.

As I contemplated the poison moving through my body, Jasper hopped off the truck bed.

He looked towards the edge of the yard, behind the barn. "What the hell is that?"

As far as I was concerned, whatever *that* was, *that* could get by just fine without me or my friend.

Jasper disagreed.

"Grady. Get over here," he said, and he reached back into the truck bed, grabbed me by my right ankle, and pulled me towards him a foot and a half.

I sat up slow and careful, not wanting to rush into another puke missile. Jasper pointed in the same direction he'd been looking – towards the edge of the yard, behind the barn. Some tall weeds grew back there between the building and the weathered wooden fence row that ringed the property, weeds tall enough to brush the eyebrows on a seventh grader or the belt buckle on a full grown man. On the other side of the fence, an open field extended a few hundred yards before the ground took a turn upward and formed a knobby hillside, pockmarked with scraggly bushes and beetle-infested pine trees.

From my position, nothing looked out of the ordinary. "What is it?" I asked Jasper.

"Look. Over there," he said, still pointing towards the yard between the fence and the barn. "See?"

I looked again. "I don't know what you're talking about."

"Come here." He grabbed me by the shoulder, pushed me directly in line with his point of view. I still couldn't see anything.

But then… I did.

Over there in the waist-high weeds, along the ground right up against the fence, some unrecognizable thing moved. Not any huge motion, for sure, but real motion no less. The tops of the weeds broke back and forth just so, enough that you knew something was in the midst of them, but not enough that you could actually make out its identity for certain.

"You see it now?" whispered Jasper.

"Yeah. Why are you whispering?"

"Because I don't want it to hear us. Why else would I be whispering?"

He had a point. "You think we ought to go check it out?" I asked, knowing full well how he'd answer.

"Of course I think we should go check it out. I've already got a pretty good idea of what it is, though –"

"Already?"

"Yeah. If you think about it long enough you'll figure it out."

"Why don't you just tell me?"

"Because that wouldn't be much fun now, would it? Come on, Grady. Think about it."

I kicked the last few hours around in my brain. But all the alcohol I'd put in my body kept my memory from pulling focus.

Jasper nodded his head towards that same corner of the weed-choked fence row that he'd been pointing at for the last little while.

"It's Raleigh." He let that thought hang in the air for a moment. "It's Raleigh Peak, sure as the world. I bet he's got one or both of those ball players on the ground. I just bet he does."

"What makes you think such a thing?" I asked. I'd barely gotten the words out when the issued was settled for good.

Raleigh Peak raised up out of the weeds.

Looked right at me and Jasper.

And I'll be damned if his whole face wasn't covered in dark red blood. Even with the combination of moonlight and liquor hanging over my head, I could see him and there wasn't any doubt about it.

I suppose the sight shocked me sober.

Not only was it Raleigh Peak, not only was his face covered in blood, but his eyes were black as 8-balls in their sockets. His mouth was wide open, too, blood streaming across his lips and teeth, into the maw and down the throat.

And the teeth. The teeth. The teeth. They jutted from the top of his mouth, one on each side, four inches long at least. Could have been a foot and a half, hell, I don't know. In between those two daggers was a row of shorter razors in the top and bottom of his mouth, serious business in their own right.

"Here we go again," sighed Jasper. "Zombies ain't enough. Witches ain't enough. Banshees ain't enough. Now we got this shit to deal with."

"You got any ideas?" I said.

"Sure. I got ideas," said Jasper. "Come on."

He headed towards Raleigh. I followed right behind him, every hint of intoxication I'd felt just a few minutes before now vanished. It's weird, how easily the combination of adrenaline and fear can wipe the cobwebs from your mind.

Raleigh never moved, just sat there with his mouth open and bloody, watching as we came his way. As we got closer I heard mournful whimpers and gurgles, the painful sounds of mortal wounds.

When we got within two or three yards I saw that Jasper had been right, indeed. Raleigh'd been at Ben Colan and Jason Kirby.

The ballplayers lay on the ground, big messy gashes ripped away from their necks, lifeblood bubbling from ripped carotid arteries. Their faces and chests were soaked in red.

Raleigh never moved. Instead, he watched us.

We stopped where we stood, seven or eight feet away. For the first time, I realized that his shirt had been torn away, and that squatting down in the weeds, with his legs out of sight, he looked naked. He looked like a snake, too, like a cobra, upright with black eyes staring at me and Jasper and those long daggers hanging from the top of his mouth, human blood still dripping off the tips.

"He's waiting for us to get closer," I whispered to Jasper. "He's gonna jump at us."

"He can hear you," he said.

"He can't hear me. I'm whispering. We're not closing enough for him to hear –"

"He can. I'd bet on it."

Jasper stood there for another moment. He stretched his right hand out in front of him, as if that might keep Raleigh at bay if he decided to jump.

"Do you think he's a vampire?" I asked.

"Nah," said Raleigh. "He's just some hungry something or another."

I thought, *He rips throats and drinks blood and charmed those poor boys into going outside where he could get 'em. What makes you think he's not a vampire?*

Before I could move the words from my brain to my mouth, Jasper lunged forward.

I thought we were dead for sure.

But as it turned out, Raleigh Peak wasn't nearly as tough as he looked. As soon as Jasper jumped at him, Raleigh let out a hiss – again I thought of a cobra – and leaped off the bodies of the basketball players, then sprung across that fence with ease and took off up the hill.

He was ten steps ahead of us before we got over the fence ourselves. But once we made it across, we got up to full speed pretty quickly. Even though the creature was moving at a good clip – I started thinking of it as a creature now, not Raleigh Peak, because it was just hard to think of something like that as human in the slightest way – he bounced around side to side a bit as he made his way up the incline, while we ran straight forward after him.

That let us gain some ground.

We chased the little bastard to the top of the hill and started down the other side without any break in stride. I got winded quickly, but Jasper never slowed, just came over the crest of the hill and kept running. That meant I kept running, too.

Moving downhill, we managed to close the gap. He kept zigging and zagging, like a jackrabbit, and we kept running that straight line, and before long Jasper got close enough that he tackled the thing from behind.

Now, listen. I'm not saying it was the smart thing to do, Jasper pulling down a monster that had just ripped apart two healthy young men without having any sort of plan to deal with that monster once they got on the ground together. I'm just saying that's what he did. Jasper got the idea in his head that we should grab him, so we grabbed him.

Jasper wrapped his arms around Raleigh's legs and brought him to the ground. As they rolled around, Raleigh gnashed his teeth, spraying spit and blood, and Jasper planted one forearm under his chin, which kept those teeth at bay but which also sent Raleigh into a wild fit as he tried and failed over and over again to sink his fangs into his prey. He could see the prey – Jasper – just inches away but he couldn't quite reach it. That didn't go over well.

I arrived on the scene about the time Jasper got that shirtless bastard flipped over on his back. As my friend held all his weight under the jaws of the beast, I jumped in.

Literally.

As soon I was near enough to do it, I leaped on Raleigh's head with both feet. Landed crossways across his face, one heel across his nose and the other across his forehead. With a sick crunch, his skull gave way like a cardboard box, and before I really had time to process what happened, I was ankle deep in his busted face.

Raleigh looked up at me, eyes wide. "Are you all right? Man oh man. You just stomped Raleigh Peak's head in."

I stepped out of the crushed skull, feet now covered in gory chunks of brain and bone. "I didn't mean to," I said, wiping my shoes off on the dry summer grass. "I was just trying to slow him down for you.

"What was I gonna do with him?"

"Maybe you should have thought about that before you took off after him." I took a breath. "Anyway, he's dead now."

"I reckon so," Jasper said. He rolled off of Raleigh's body and stood up. Something on the ground caught his attention, and when I looked in that same direction I saw it was another pill bottle. And another. And another. By the time I finished, I counted twelve of them all, each one filled to the top with little red capsules, just like the pill bottle he'd given Ben and Jason in the barn.

Jasper bent down and picked up one of the bottles, helt it flat in his open palm. "You know what I think?" he said. "I think he was trading. Only those two guys didn't seem exactly aware of what it was they were trading away to him."

The drug problems that we'd seen move in to Whistle Mill in the last few years made so much more sense now.

HARBINGERS

The Raleigh Peak incident happened in the last summer before we were expected to join what under normal circumstances would be called "the real world."

But with everything we'd experienced, me and Jasper knew better. For us, the world of college classes and forty hour work weeks was no more "real" than the Boone Creek banshee or the Lady of the Woods or the Walters family and their scheme trading pills for the blood children.

After Evie's, I actually didn't see Jasper the rest of June. That was without a doubt the longest we'd gone without hanging out in all the time we'd been friends.

He stayed around his house most the time, and I stayed around mine. We talked on the phone from time to time but never could quite get together, what with all the prep for college and maybe just the general feeling that high school graduation was one of those milestones that should be followed by significant Change in the lives of all involved. Like in those movies where the circle of childhood friends pinky promises that they'll stick together no matter what the mean ol' world throws at them, only to find out the world's got a few bad ass magic tricks in the bag that *nobody* saw coming, and pretty much everybody ends up on drugs or dead or (most likely) both.

That's one thing everybody learns as you get older: life comes at us all, and more often than not, it comes *between* us all. Maybe not a hundred percent, maybe not even half that. But one thing you can write down in your little diaries, kids: all those friends you grew up with, all the ones you spent every weekend with and made all those big plans with, you all eventually find out that there are a few more forks in the road than you anticipated when you were playing together on the playground with GI Joes.

You thought you'd always make time for them and they'd always make time for you, but as everybody learns, there's just not enough time to be made. Even for the best, closest of friends. Even for friends like me and Jasper Bohanon. It happens. That's the truth.

I can't say if, subconsciously, the two of us already felt time and life creeping between us, but looking back on it now I do wonder if maybe that's true. Maybe we started drifting apart that summer on our own accord, before forces beyond our control took over. Who knows?

All I can say is, me and Jasper didn't talk much during that June and July. And whether we realized it or not, we were readying ourselves for the next stage of our lives, Him off for more school, me off to... somewhere. I still didn't know where.

But wherever it was, I knew that I wouldn't have Jasper there, walking with me in the darkness the way he'd walked with me ever since we first met that fateful recess one day in fifth grade at Whistle Mill Elementary. He'd had a handful of G.I. Joes. Duke, Destro, and two Cobra soldiers, to be exact. Destro had a loose waist and flopped around like a marionette. I still remember that. He loved comic books and horror movies and *Fangoria* magazine, and that got us through a lot of years together.

How much longer did we have? Who can ever really say?

That 4th of July, I called Jasper's house. His Mom said he'd gone out of town for a few days. That surprised me, his leaving the area like that without even the barest mention of where he was going and when he might be back. But, hey. Time, Life, and all that.

But, a couple of days after that phone call with Mrs. Bohanon, I got a letter in the mail that explained everything.

Hey Grady,

Hope you're having a great summer. Don't tell me if you aren't, okay?

First of all, I'm sorry we haven't had much chance to get together in the last couple of weeks; I've had a lot to do in getting ready to head out West, and I didn't think you'd find it all that interesting. It's a lot of paperwork shuffling, clothes buying, and map reading, trying to get familiar with the lay of the land. Of course I won't rally get a good feel for it all until I actually get *there, live and in stereo, but hey, I'd rather not walk into it completely blind.*

Be that as it may, for the last few days I've put college out of my mind. Been visiting my Aunt Jackie and Uncle John's place here in Hopkinsville. Well, not really Hopkinsville proper – maybe ten miles outside of town, to be exact. Jackie is my dad's younger sister. They've got a daughter who's currently in school at Murray State, and a son, Max, who's our age. The family are "good people" as you hear a lot around these parts. Uncle John's got a rebel flag painted across his garage door. He don't mean anything insulting about it. I asked him if he knew what it stood for and he just laughed, said, "It stands for I don't by-God take shit off anybody."

Well, then.

Max is a different sort than you and me. More – how do you say? – grounded. He likes to listen to Pearl Jam and some of those other Seattle bands (you know I never really cared much for that) and dick around on his pick-up truck engine. He's not too worried about Infinity and the things that live in the darkness, the way you and I have been. I'm not saying he's better or worse off for it, now. Just that's how he is.

All the time I've been out here, we haven't really gotten into a whole lot, just some fishing and dirt bike riding. He figured out in the first couple of days of the visit that I wasn't going to be much help on that truck of his, and so he decided maybe we ought to spend the 4ᵗʰ of July over at Lake Barkley. You know, put the boat out and ride around and see what happened.

Aunt Jackie and Uncle John have a cabin on the lake, and we figured we could spend a night or two over there. Max said he could get us some beer if I wanted, knows a guy at one of the liquor stores that don't mind slipping some to a friend for a couple extra bucks cash money. I tried to tell him that I wasn't a fan of beer or alcohol in general, but we ended up with a case of Milwaukee's Best anyway. The beer of kings.

Now, here's where it gets interesting.

When we first got to the cabin, it was almost too dark out to see, and by the time Max got through that case of Milwaukee's Best, the sun was long gone and a thick bank of clouds blanked out the stars and promised a heckuva storm on the way. We flipped on the television and sure enough, there was a severe thunderstorm warning out. The weatherman even said that storm watchers had spotted a funnel cloud two counties west.

"You think we ought to stick it out here?" I asked Max. "I'd hate to get caught out in a mess like that," I said. "And it surely will be a mess."

"Fine. Let's stay here," Max said, already feeling the beer's effects. "Call my mom, let her know. Phone's in the kitchen."

Good enough for me. I didn't much care for the idea of riding back with a drunk, anyway.

I got the phone, called Aunt Jackie and let her know we'd be home soon as the storm passed. That suited her just fine. I doubt it would have suited her just fine knowing that her son was shit hammered and soon to be passed out on the couch, but since she didn't ask to speak to him, I didn't volunteer that particular status update.

Less fifteen minutes after I hung up the phone, the wind kicked up and lightning flashed behind the distant hills on the west side of Lake Barkley. Thunder growled low and weak at first, but as the storm blew that turned up the volume and the lightning that provided a gentle *backlight to the clouds became jagged streaks of blue-white, ripping towards the ground.*

On the television, the weatherman broke into programming and announced that the thunderstorm was strengthening and residents in the path should go to an interior room where they could stay away from all windows until it passed. Ignoring his professional advice, I stood next to the bay window that dominated the cabin's living room and watched the atmosphere crackle outside the glass.

I always did love a good storm. You know it, Grady. A good storm always makes me think about whatever might be Out There, the forces we can't see or control no matter how hard we try. The forces that wait for us in the infinite darkness, just like you and I always talked about.

After a particularly vicious thunder boom, I heard a crash above my head.

A tree limb smacked the roof, *I thought. Seemed obvious enough.*

Then, I heard the same thing again.

And again.

"Hey, Max. Did you hear that?" I asked.

When Max didn't answer, I turned around and saw he'd completed his crossover into alcohol-induced unconsciousness, laying asleep with his face crammed back into the corner of the couch. That meant we were staying for the night, regardless of how long the storm lasted. There was no way in hell I could take Max back to his parents with him smelling like a brewery. They'd have his ass for sure, and probably mine, too.

Whatever was on the roof, I figured I'd just let it go until after the storm finished, then go check to see if there was any real damage to the house (we'd have to let my aunt and uncle know about that, for sure).

I went back into the kitchen to see if I could rustle up anything to eat. As I scrounged through first the refrigerator and then the cabinets – without any luck – I heard another thump *upstairs.*

Several thump*s.*

Thump.

Thump.

Thump.

But these were different than what I'd heard earlier. These didn't sound like fallen tree limbs. They reminded me of being at my grandparents with all my cousins, and being downstairs while the rest of the kids played upstairs.

One.

Two.

Three.

Four.

Intermittent at first. Then closer together.

One Two.

Three Four.

Five Six.

Then all at once. And louder.

ONETWOTHREEFOURFIVESIX

It sounded like… footsteps. Like somebody running on the roof. First one person. Then many.

I hustled over to the staircase and ran up to the second floor. Before I was halfway there, I heard several more thumps, but this time they were downstairs, *coming at the front wall of the house, in the vicinity of the bay window where I'd been standing just a few moments before.*

Then they were upstairs again.

Downstairs.

Then upstairs and *downstairs at the same time.*

My blood pumped hard now. I couldn't see what was making all that noise on top of and around the outside of the cabin.

But I knew for sure it wasn't any busted damn tree limbs.

In that moment, I felt the very same sensation that I felt on the other adventures we've shared — the night with that witch Ms. Stanton up Martin Holler, the run-in with Raleigh Peak, the damned banshee of Boone Creek that got your Uncle Ted.

Adrenaline poured through my body, opening my eyes, turning up the volume in my ears.

Lights flared outside. Red, green, blue, starbursts shining from above, all the way to the ground.

As those lights flared around the outside of the cabin, I heard something that I can only describe as laughter. Not the laughter of happiness, or even insanity, but the laughter of children.

Children playing.

I couldn't see what set on us that night, but we definitely had visitors at the cabin on Lake Barkley.

After an hour or so, the thumping noises stopped, and I didn't see or hear anything else the rest of the night. When Max woke up the next morning, I told him what happened and he got real excited, and decided that we had to stay over a little longer. Which we did.

The next night, the noises returned.

So did the lights.

And so did the laughter. The unsettling laughter of a hundred children, playing together, just out of sight from the adults in the other room…

But that night, I finally saw where the laughter and the lights and the footsteps on the roof all came from.

We've got visitors, Grady. They aren't exactly Hopkinsville locals, either. They've been here every night and I know they'll still be visiting whenever you get here.

Just give me a call when you get this letter, will you? It makes a better story out loud.

As always,
Jasper

P.S.,
I know I could have called and told you all of this over the telephone, but it's much more fun reading about it in letters, don't you think? Just like in the old days. (Letter writing is an art form and I hope it never dies.)

I folded Jasper's letter back into the envelope, and tucked it away in the top drawer of my desk, the same single-drawer pine desk that had stood in the corner of my bedroom since middle school. The thought crossed my mind that I should call Jasper, but both of us knew that there wasn't a damn thing on Earth could keep me from joining him in Hopkinsville just as soon as I figured out a way to get there.

That trip was a few hours away, though. In the meantime, I needed to get back into the right frame of mind for the looming adventure.

I scanned my bookshelf, searching through shelves bowed with the weight of nearly two decades' worth of horror and science fiction experience. The names of masters and their greatest works rolled by, old friends all. *Star Wars. The Empire Strikes Back. Return of the Jedi. Star Trek.*

The Wrath of Khan. The Search for Spock. The Voyage Home. Friday the 13th. A Nightmare on Elm Street. Isaac Asimov. *Foundation Trilogy.* Stephen King. *The Stand. It. 'Salem's Lot. The Eyes of the Dragon. Night Shift. Skeleton Crew.* Steven Spielberg. *Raiders of the Lost Ark. E.T. Temple of Doom.* David Cronenberg. *The Fly. Scanners.* Dan Simmons. H.P. Lovecraft. Joe Lansdale. *Robocop. Predator. The Terminator. Aliens. Creepshow.*

So many.

X-men comics. *The New Mutants. Amazing Spider-man. ROM: Spaceknight. Micronauts. Secret Wars.*

So many.

Fangoria magazine.

Fangoria.

Fangoria.

Fangoria.

So many.

One of the *Fangoria* stacks caught my eye, at the end of the shelf that was closest to my bed. On top of the stack was that Holy Grail, issue number nine, with *Motel Hell.* The issue banned immediately after publication by the church ladies and Reaganistas with their Brylcreem and their pompadours and their granny diapers and their crazed, self-righteous fervor. I mentioned it earlier: that farmer dude in denim overalls and red flannel shirt, wearing a pig's head for a helmet, wielding a bloody chainsaw like it was the mighty Excalibur or something.

Far as I was concerned, human hands weren't capable of creating a more badass cover. I believed it in elementary school and I believed it at that moment, years later. Probably they still aren't.

Fangoria number nine was the one issue that caught my eye eight years earlier, on that October day in 1985 when I first met Jasper Bohanon on the playground of Whistle Mill Elementary. I knew that any kid who'd gotten their hands on that issue – and had the balls to bring it with them to school, along with a backpack full of other *Fangoria*s and comic books – was bound to be somebody that I could get on board with. And was he ever.

Me and Jasper have been on fantastic adventures from Whistle Mill to Hopkinsville, Kentucky to California, and even Heaven to Hell and back – literally! – and I've had my eyes opened about this world and other worlds, too, in ways that everybody ought to experience. But of all the moments we shared, the one that I hold closest to this day happened just a couple years after we met, during one of the many weekends that we happily frittered away on a *Friday the 13th* movie marathon.

The weekend Jasper pulled that *Fangoria* number nine out of his backpack, and handed it to me.

"Hey, Boo," he said. "You want this or what?"

I didn't believe him at first. "Seriously?"

"Hell yeah, I'm serious," said Jasper.

"Why on Earth would you want to give that away?"

"Take it." That's all he said, reaching it further towards me. Then he added, "I got another."

Now, I don't know if he truly did have another copy. That issue was rare enough that part of me found it hard to believe he'd have not one but *two* of them. Maybe he was just saying that to make me feel better about taking his offer. But then again, if anybody could possess two *Fangoria* number nines, Jasper Bohanon could do it. That was for damn sure.

"Go ahead. It's yours," he said.

I took it.

Number nine went home with me, I read through once, then put it into a Mylar sleeve for safe keeping, just like I did with all my favorite issues. The one with that *Maximum Overdrive* Green Goblin truck on the cover, the one with *The Fly*, the one with *Lost Boys,* the one with *Predator* which all factors considered is probably the single best issue of *Fangoria* ever put together so far as actual content goes. And in that Mylar sleeve it stayed.

After reading Jasper's letter from Hopkinsville and thinking about what we might get into down there, I picked up that special issue for the first time since the day my friend gave it to me. I considered opening it and thumbing through the pages, breathing in the fragrance of old paper and ink that is so familiar to collectors.

I couldn't bring myself to do it, though. Number nine seemed sacred, a historical relic too valuable for mere mortal hands.

Back on the shelf it went.

My mind raced with thoughts of what I might find in Hopkinsville. Something weird had visited Jasper and his cousin Max at the cabin, no doubt about it. I couldn't contain the excitement of seeing for myself; I didn't even *want* to contain it. I may not have had a car of my own, but I'd find a way to get down there. I *had* to find a way.

For now, out the window, night in Whistle Mill slept clean and clear, and quiet as a monastery. No banshee, no Lady of the Woods anywhere to be seen. No bloodthirsty creatures, reanimated corpses, or other such travelers in the darkness. Just an empty night. A still night.

I stared into the stars. They blinked back against the infinite backdrop that me and Jasper had discussed so many times, a celestial reminder of all the possibilities the great universe held for anyone willing to look up and see them.

"Infinity ain't a point on a line," he told me once. "It's *every* point on *every* line. It's possibility, that's what it is. Naw, hell, it's more than that. It's *all* possibilities."

There were so many lines in front of us, so many points along them. What waited for us out there, exactly? I didn't know. I *couldn't* know. The one truth – maybe the only truth – I ever knew for sure is that no friend in this world could face down unnatural forces with the strength and conviction of my friend Jasper Bohanon. And how. Me and Jasper, we've seen a hell of a lot of weirdness in our ninety-something years together on this planet, but as long as I had him at my back it felt like we could pull through just about anything.

And we did, too. We just about did.

It might go against mankind's common instinct to say this, but then again me and Jasper never did consider ourselves the common sort, so saying it's just what I'm gonna do. In my adventures with Jasper Bohanon – the adventures we've had already and the adventures I know we'll find soon enough – I've learned a single fact above all others: there's things out there in the shadows, waiting on us. Cold things. Dead things. Awful, evil things, things that reach out from the shadows and grab your throat, things that would just as soon shred the skin from your bones as look at you with their one good eye. Things damned to hell forever. Things that ain't supposed to be real. Things that would stay out of the light forever if most men had their way.

But me and Jasper, we aren't most men.

This is the story of how we walked in the darkness...

TO BE CONTINUED.

Coming soon!

Adventures in Terror: Mostly the 21st Century

Featuring:

Me and Jasper and the Return of the Hopkinsville Goblins

Me and Jasper and the Creepy Kids

Homer and Henry Finally Get Their Revenge

Maximum Overdrive 2

Me and Jasper and the Infinite Madness

Me and Jasper and Midnight Blue

Motel Hell 2

Me and Jasper and the Last Night in Gatlinburg

Somewhere Between Heaven and Hell

And more! So much more!

APPENDIX A

Me and Jasper do hereby recommend the following books and authors, taken from the same time period as the setting for this volume of *Adventures in Terror*. Not all of said authors' books are listed – explore further on your own!

STEPHEN KING:
'Salem's Lot (1975)
The Stand (1978)
Night Shift (1978)
The Long Walk (1979, as Richard Bachman)
Cujo (1981)
Danse Macabre (1981)
Christine (1983)
Pet Sematary (1983)
Cycle of the Werewolf (1983)
The Talisman (1984, with Peter Straub)
It (1986)
The Eyes of the Dragon (1987)
Misery (1987)
The Dark Half (1989)

JOE LANSDALE:
*The Drive-In: A "B" Movie with Blood and Popcorn,
    Made in Texas* (1988)
The Drive-In 2: Not Just One of Them Sequels (1989)

DAN SIMMONS:
The Song of Kali (1985)
Carrion Comfort (1989)

Summer of Night (1991)

JOHN SKIPP AND CRAIG SPECTOR:
The Light at the End (1986)
The Clean-up (1987)

CLIVE BARKER:
Books of Blood (1984-1985)

PETER STRAUB:
Ghost Story (1979)
Floating Dragon (1983)
The Talisman (1984, with Stephen King)

ROBERT MCCAMMON:
Swan Song (1987)
Stinger (1988)

RAMSEY CAMPBELL
The Parasite (1980)
Obsession (1985)
Scared Stiff: Tales of Sex and Death (1987)
Ancient Images (1989)
Midnight Sun (1990)

JANET MORRIS, editor:
Heroes in Hell (1986)
Rebels in Hell (1986)

THOMAS HARRIS:
Red Dragon (1981)
The Silence of the Lambs (1988)

CHARLES L. GRANT:
Night Songs (1984)
The Dark Cry of the Moon (1986)
The Long Night of the Grave (1986)

F. PAUL WILSON:
The Keep (1981)
The Tomb (1984)

JOHN SAUL
Suffer the Children (1977)
Punish the Sinners (1978)
Brain Child (1985)
The Unwanted (1987)
Creature (1989)

V.C. ANDREWS
Flowers in the Attic (1979)

BEN BOVA
Test of Fire (1982)
The Winds of Altair (1983)

ORSON SCOTT CARD
Ender's Game (1985)
Seventh Son (1987)

All of the above did great work from 1975-1993, and many were great well after that. Then we have the guys below, literary giants from earlier in the 20th century, who laid the groundwork for all that came after. Perhaps you've heard of some of these:

H.P. LOVECRAFT
At the Mountains of Madness (1931)
The Shadow over Innsmouth (1931)
The Colour Out of Space (1927)
The Shadow Out of Time (1935)
The Case of Charles Dexter Ward (1927)
"The Call of Cthulhu" (1926)
"The Rats in the Walls" (1923)
"Dagon" (1917)
"Herbert West—Reanimator" (1921)
"Pickman's Model" (1926)
"The Dunwich Horror" (1928)
"The Music of Erich Zann" (1921)
"The Outsider" (1921
"The Whisperer in Darkness" (1930)
"The Horror at Red Hook" (1925)

ROBERT BLOCH
Psycho (1959)
Night of the Ripper (1984)
Yours Truly, Jack the Ripper (1962)
Nightmares (1961)

RAY BRADBURY
Something Wicked This Way Comes (1962)
The Martian Chronicles (1950)
Dandelion Wine (1957)
Fahrenheit 451 (1953)
Dark Carnival (1947)

PHILIP K. DICK
Do Androids Dream of Electric Sleep? (1966)
The Man in the High Castle (1961)
The Gameplayers of Titan (1963)
Ubik (1969)
A Scanner Darkly (1977)
The Three Stigmata of Palmer Eldritch (1965)

ISAAC ASIMOV
I, Robot (1950)
Foundation (1951)
Foundation and Empire (1952)
Second Foundation (1953)
Foundation's Edge (1982)
The Intelligent Man's Guide to Science (1960)
Nightfall and Other Stories (1969)
The Bicentennial Man and Other Stories (1976)

ARTHUR C. CLARKE
2001: A Space Odyssey (1968)
Rendezvous with Rama (1972)
Childhood's End (1953)
Prelude to Space (1951)
The Fountains of Paradise (1979)

H.G. WELLS
The Time Machine (1895)
The War of the Worlds (1898)
The Invisible Man (1897)
The Island of Dr. Moreau (1896)
The First Men in the Moon (1901)

JULES VERNE
Twenty Thousand Leagues under the Sea (1869)
From the Earth to the Moon (1865)
Journey to the Center of the Earth (1864)
Around the World in Eighty Days (1872)

BRAM STOKER
Dracula (1897)
The Jewel of Seven Stars (1903)
The Lady of the Shroud (1909)
The Lair of the White Worm (1911)

APPENDIX B

Me and Jasper also recommend these fine horror and science fiction movies, also from the same time period as this volume of *Adventures in Terror*. Many of the VHS boxes will forever be burned into my memory.

The list is nowhere near complete, but it'll set you down the right road.

Friday the 13th (1980), dir. Sean Cunningham
Friday the 13th Part 2 (1981), dir. Steve Miner
Friday the 13th Part 3 (1982), dir. Steve Miner
Friday the 13th the Final Chapter (1984), dir.
  Joseph Zito
Friday the 13th Part V: A New Beginning (1985), dir.
  Danny Steinman
Friday the 13th Part VI: Jason Lives (1986), dir.
  Tom McLoughlin
Friday the 13th Part VII: The New Blood (1988), dir.
  John Carl Buechler
Friday the 13th Part VIII: Jason Takes Manhattan
  (1989), dir. Rob Hedden
Jason Goes to Hell (a.k.a. *Friday the 13th Part IX)*
  *(*1993), dir. Adam Marcus
A Nightmare on Elm Street (1984*)*, dir. Wes Craven
A Nightmare on Elm Street 3: Dream Warriors (1987),
  dir. Chuck Russell
*Halloween (*1978*)*, dir. John Carpenter

Halloween II (1981), dir. Rick Rosenthal
Halloween III (1982), dir. Tommy Lee Wallace
The Thing (1982), dir. John Carpenter
The Fog (1980), dir. John Carpenter
Big Trouble in Little China (1986), dir.
  John Carpenter
Prince of Darkness (1987), dir. John Carpenter
Poltergeist (1982), dir. Tobe Hooper
House by the Cemetery (1981), dir. Lucio Fulci
City of the Living Dead (1980), dir. Lucio Fulci
The Beyond (1981), dir. Lucio Fulci
The Beast Within (1982), dir. Phillipe Mora
Motel Hell (1980) dir. Kevin Connor
Wolfen (1981), dir. Michael Wadleigh
Re-Animator (1985), dir. Stuart Gordon
From Beyond (1986), dir. Stuart Gordon
Suspiria (1977), dir. Dario Argento
Scanners (1981), dir. David Cronenberg
*Videodrome (*1983), dir. David Cronenberg
The Fly (1986), dir. David Cronenberg
The Lost Boys (1987), dir. Joel Schumacher
Pumpkinhead (1988), dir. Stan Winston
ALIENS (1986), dir. James Cameron
Robocop (1987), dir. Paul Verhoeven
Total Recall (1990) dir. Paul Verhoeven
Gremlins (1984), dir. Joe Dante
Angel Heart (1987), dir. Alan Parker
Maximum Overdrive (1986), dir. Stephen King
Creepshow (1982), dir. George Romero
Creepshow 2 (1987), dir. Michael Gornick
The Last Starfighter (1984), dir. Nick Castle
*The Adventures of Buckaroo Banzai across the 8th
  Dimension* (1984), dir. W.D. Richter

Dressed to Kill (1980), dir. Brian De Palma
Body Double (1984), dir. Brian De Palma
My Bloody Valentine (1981), dir. George Mihalka
House of the Long Shadows (1983), dir. Pete Walker
Blood Diner (1987), dir. Jackie Kong
Pieces (1982), dir. Juan Piquer Simon
Raiders of the Lost Ark (1981), dir. Steven Spielberg
Indiana Jones and the Temple of Doom (1984), dir.
   Steven Spielberg
Indiana Jones and the Last Crusade (1989), dir.
   Steven Spielberg
Star Wars (1977), dir. George Lucas
The Empire Strikes Back (1980), dir.
   Irving Kershner
Return of the Jedi (1983), dir. Richard Marquand
The Terminator (1984), dir. James Cameron
Star Trek II: The Wrath of Khan (1982), dir.
   Nicholas Meyer
Star Trek III: The Search for Spock (1984), dir.
   Leonard Nimoy
Star Trek IV: The Voyage Home (1986), dir.
   Leonard Nimoy
Aliens Deadly Spawn (a.k.a. *The Deadly Spawn*),
   (1983) dir. Douglas McKeown
The Serpent and the Rainbow (1987), dir. Wes Craven
C.H.U.D. (1984), dir. Douglas Cheek
The Burning (1981), dir. Tony Maylam
An American Werewolf in London (1981), dir.
   John Landis
Dead and Buried (1981), dir. Gary Sherman
The Evil Dead (1981), dir. Sam Raimi
Evil Dead 2 (1987), dir. Sam Raimi
The Howling (1981), dir. Joe Dante

Fright Night (1985), dir. Tom Holland

The Stuff (1985), dir. Larry Cohen

Henry: Portrait of a Serial Killer (1986), dir.
  John McNaughton

Bad Taste (1987), dir. Peter Jackson

Hellraiser (1987), dir. Clive Barker

The Blob (1988), dir. Chuck Russell

Metalstorm: The Destruction of Jared Syn (1983), dir.
  Charles Band

Krull (1983), dir. Peter Yates

The Dorm that Dripped Blood (1982), dir.
  Stephen Carpenter/Jeffrey Obrow

The Bogey Man (1980), dir. Ulli Lommel

Critters (1986), dir. Stephen Herek

Subspecies (1991), dir. Ted Nicolau

Mad Max (1979), dir. George Miller

The Road Warrior (1981), dir. George Miller

Mad Max Beyond Thunderdome (1985), dir.
  George Miller

Predator (1987), dir. John McTiernan

The Running Man (1987), dir.

Alligator (1980), dir. Lewis Teague

Demons (1985), dir. Lamberto Bava

The Church (1989), dir. Michael Soavi

Deadly Friend (1986), dir. Wes Craven

Trick or Treat (1986), dir. Charles Martin Smith

Happy Birthday to Me (1981), dir. J. Lee Thompson

Hell Night (1981), dir. Tom DeSimone

Ice Pirates (1984), dir. Stewart Raffill

Jaws 3-D (1983), dir. Joe Alves

Time Bandits (1981), dir. Terry Gilliam

Trancers (1985), dir. Charles Band

Eliminators (1986), dir. Peter Manoogian

The Borrower (1991), dir. John McNaughton
Waxwork (1988), dir. Anthony Hickox
Waxwork II (1992), dir. Anthony Hickox
The Neverending Story (1984), dir.
  Wolfgang Peterson
Escape from New York (1981), dir. John Carpenter
Nosferatu the Vampire (1979), dir. Werner Herzog
Candyman (1992), dir. Bernard Rose
Anguish (1987), dir. Bigas Luna
Leviathan (1989), dir. George P. Cosmatos
Return of the Living Dead (1985), dir.
  Dan O'Bannon
Texas Chainsaw Massacre 2 (1986), dir.
  Tobe Hooper
Poltergeist II: The Other Side (1986), dir.
  Brian Gibson
Stand by Me (1986), dir. Rob Reiner
The Zero Boys (1986), dir. Nico Mastorakis
Bill and Ted's Excellent Adventure (1989), dir.
  Stephen Herek
Bill and Ted's Bogus Journey (1991), dir. Peter Hewitt
The Unnamable (1988), dir. Jean-Paul Ouellette
Day of the Dead (1985), dir. George Romero
Death Spa (1989), dir. Michael Fischa
Little Shop of Horrors (1986), dir. Frank Oz
Xtro (1982), dir. Harry Bromley Davenport
Spasms (1983), dir. William Fruett
Terror Train (1980), dir. Roger Spottiswoode
Prom Night (1980), dir. Paul Lynch
Phantasm (1979), dir. Don Coscarelli
Phantasm II (1988), dir. Don Coscarelli
The Fury (1978), dir. Brian DePalma
TRON (1982), dir. Steven Lisberger

The Company of Wolves (1984), dir. Neil Jordan
Altered States (1980), dir. Ken Russell
The Lair of the White Worm (1988), dir. Ken Russell
Inferno (1980), dir. Dario Argento
Opera (1987), dir. Dario Argento
Legend (1985), dir. Ridley Scott
The Dark Crystal (1982), dir. Jim Henson/
  Frank Oz
Labyrinth (1986), dir. Jim Henson

AUTHOR'S NOTES

Allow me to indulge myself with some self-important final discussion. Inside baseball, as they call it. I have always loved those "making of" documentaries that accompany so many movie discs, and I suppose the last few pages of this book are my version of that. If you're not like me and you don't care about "that shit," feel free to close the book now.

But just know, if you do close the book right this very second, it's your loss, not mine.

First off, a few words about my dear friend Steven Goldmann, to whom *Adventures in Terror: Mostly the 1980s* is dedicated, and who departed this Earth after a long fight against multiple myeloma on April 30, 2015 – just as I was finishing up the story you're reading now.

From where I stand, he fought like a motherfucker. He told me enough stories about his battles with cancer to prove beyond all doubt that he was a numero uno badass. Steven would have made Jasper Bohanon and Grady Claremont oh so proud. He made a lot of people proud, I'll tell you that much, which you can see for yourself through a quick search of the various Googles and Facebooks and Yahoos and whatever other mystical interwebs exist out there.

I'm sorry that he never got to read this book. He would have loved it. I held out hope that I could send him these adventures of Jasper and Grady and that it would cheer him up just a little, and I was writing hard in those last days for that reason if nothing else, but I came up short. Alas.

The day Steven died, I posted a short tribute on my website. It's not likely that I could say anything better about my friend than what I said that day, so I'll say it again here:

We always joked about how crazy it was that a Jewish guy from Montreal and a heathen from the hills of Eastern Kentucky could think so much alike, but we did. We really did. Politics, movies, music, *Fangoria* magazine. Whatever. We weren't 100% on everything - he used to marvel at how much Ale-8 I drank and I used to marvel at how much time it must have taken him to get his hair ready in the morning - but we shared way more interests than you'd ever guess from our backgrounds. He was the first person outside of "back home" that ever stood up for my writing; I sold him the screenplay for *The Rassler* and even though that story like so many other great stories has never quite made it to the lighted screen, it was validation for me. It brought reassurance that I knew what I was doing. That meant a lot.

I worked for Steven for a year, and then I worked with him on myriad projects for 15 years after that, right up until his battle took its final turn in these last few months. He did so much great work. He was a real artist. He made movies, like *Trailer Park of Terror* and *Broken Bridges*). He made music videos – at his peak, he made some of the biggest in the biz, for superstars like Faith Hill, Alan Jackson, Shania Twain, and the Mavericks, among many, many others. One of our great unfulfilled projects was a movie starring the Mavericks, meant for release with their first greatest hits package and based on the Coen Brothers' absolute masterpiece *The Big Lebowski*. (If you don't know the Mavericks or *The Big Lebowski*, all I can say is obviously, you're not a golfer.)

He loved stories and he'd do everything he could to tell them, in whatever medium would let him through the door just long enough to get a good hold. I've lost count of how many different ideas we kicked around, and I was just one person that he kicked them around with. There were so many others besides me, and I'm sure that's because no one person could hope to catch all of the man's creative energy in one basket.

But he wasn't just a professional, and he wasn't just an artist. He was a kind, intelligent, and generous man. He dreamed Big and he believed Big – I think I appreciated that about Steven Goldmann more than anything else – and when he talked about his dreams he had a way of making you believe Big, too. One of the last conversations we had, he wanted to take another run at a *Sewerville* television series with me and Alan Brewer. Giving me more script notes, talking up the idea, lending it all hope. Of course he was.

*

There are a few times that *Adventures in Terror* references Ray Bradbury's classic *Something Wicked This Way Comes,* starting with the quote that opens the proceedings. ("It was in their friendship they just wanted to run forever, shadow and shadow.")

I'm telling you that right now, so those who are familiar with Bradbury's story of fantasy and friendship don't think I was trying to slip a few fast ones by you fine folks. Bradbury is a bit of a jumping off point for *Adventures in Terror* and it's not unintentional.

Jasper and Grady's birthdays – born in the same year, one a few minutes before Halloween midnight, one just a few minutes after – are shared with Jim Nightshade and Will Halloway, the two friends in Bradbury's book.

The "book" where Grady read that "no carnival comes after Labor Day... the carnival comes when it wants. On its own clock, at its own speed" and which also says that carnivals only come at dawn is, of course, *Something Wicked This Way Comes.*

Actually the entire chapter "The Carnival" is partially a tribute to that great book and author. I could never equal or even approach that masterwork and would never even try. What I *can* do is pay my respects and encourage everyone reading these words to put down this book immediately, go find a copy of *Something Wicked This Way Comes*, and enjoy. Read it for the first time. Read it for the hundredth time. Just read it. You're welcome.

*

For me, one of the most enjoyable aspects of writing this first volume of *Adventures in Terror* is that it's engaged me in a bit of universe building.

Obviously, the story is almost entirely set in fictional Seward County, Kentucky, the same Seward County where my first novel *Sewerville* takes place. Where *Sewerville* is real-world darkness and takes on topics that interest (and worry) me about this crazy little Planet Earth that certain members (?) of our dear human race have managed to turn into such a giant fiasco, it was always my intention that *Adventures in Terror* be the horror/sci-fi/fantasy flip side of that world. Grady and Jasper live on the "other" end of Seward County, and that's no accident.

Just like the boys in this story, I spent my school years on the "other" end of my county (Powell County, Kentucky). There wasn't any Whistle Mill-like town on our end, though – just some houses, farms, and the occasional country store all scattered about the wooded hills and hollows, with only a single two-lane (that sometimes was really only wide enough for one lane) highway snaking through to connect them. It wasn't really that far from the county seat of Stanton – maybe six or seven miles – but to a little kid with no sense of the world's true size, it felt like we lived in the hinterlands.

My friend Brinton Epperson and I grew up together out there. We hiked the hills from as long ago as I can remember. When we were second graders, we tore through the underbrush, swinging tobacco sticks as swords, pretending we were Greek gods. We spent most every weekend from elementary through high school at each other's houses. There were countless conversations about philosophy and science, history and politics, the Beatles and Twisted Sister. (Brinton is a Beatles man. I'll always be a hard rock guy.) Both of us even had the same car as Evie Fallon – the dreaded Olds Firenza. His was green, mine was brown. He got his a few years before I got mine but I don't think either one of us would claim we drove a sex machine.

There's an awful lot of Brinton in Jasper Bohanon, and when he reads this book I have to think he'll recognize himself.

But, there are a few other people in Jasper too, and I want to make sure they know that. Michael Saylor (my brother), David Rogers, Daylan Kinser, Anthony Gabbard, Daxon Caudill, Kevin Hall, Cory Graham, Kelly Hobbs.

Yes, I am well aware that "me and Jasper" is not correct, grammatically speaking. But it's the way I wanted it, it's the way I wrote it, and it's the way it stays until Jasper finally reaches the edge of infinity that intrigues him so.

Nyah nyah nya-nyah yahhhhhhhhh, grammar police. It's how the characters talk. Leave us the hell alone.

Randall, in "Me and Jasper and the Little Red Pills"? You either get it or you don't.

Back to the universe building.

There are several direct references to *Sewerville* – at least the town of Sewardville – which readers of that novel will recognize. It makes sense to me; the towns are in same county and I own all the real estate there.

In addition to those references, *Adventures in Terror* also exists at a crossroads with some other work that will be coming down the parkway soon enough. An older Jasper Bohanon appears in the second *Sewerville* book, *The Gentleman from Kentucky*. And the Peak family from "Me and Jasper and the Little Red Pills" are significant players in the novel *Lords of the Dark*. Both those books will likely be out within the next couple of years.

Why am I telling you this? 'Cause I want to. I enjoy it. Plenty of writers cross-pollinate their different works; I'm doing the same. Maybe it just comes down to the fact that it's plain old *fun*, having your own world in which to play. If you don't believe me, give it a try sometime.

Anyway, the aforementioned books will be out before you know it, and when they're all out there for your reading pleasure, please feel free to judge my little universe for yourself.

The next volume of *Adventures in Terror* is subtitled *Mostly the 21st Century*. It continues the story of Jasper and Grady in some ways you might expect and others that I am thinking you probably won't. Time will tell. I expect the book will see release a year or so from now and then everyone can find out together. Until then...

Aaron Saylor
Lexington KY
April 1, 2015

GOOD NIGHT.

ALSO BY AARON SAYLOR:

Sewerville: A Southern Gangster Novel

Lost Change and Loose Cousins
(with Strother Kevin Hall)

The Dead on Black River

The Sweet Smell of Pine Needles